Hubcaps
and Puppies

Rosemary Nelson

Hubcaps and Puppies

Rosemary Nelson

Napoleon Publishing

Cover art: June Lawrason

Le Conseil des Arts du Canada DEPUIS 1957 | The Canada Council for the arts SINCE 1957

We gratefully acknowledge the support of the Canada
Council for the Arts for our publishing program.

Napoleon Publishing
Toronto, Ontario, Canada
www.napoleonpublishing.com

Printed in Canada

06 05 04 03 02   5 4 3 2 1

National Library of Canada Cataloguing in Publication

Nelson, Rosemary, date-
  Hubcaps and puppies / Rosemary Nelson.

ISBN 0-929141-98-9

I. Endangered species--Juvenile fiction. I. Title.

PS8577.E39H82 2002   jC813'.54   C2002-902963-5
PZ7

For Tannis and Scott, caretakers of our planet, and Kelly and Shawn, who fill up a room with sunshine! As well, this book is dedicated to the black and white collie in the Agility Trials at the Armstrong Fair. His keenness for the sport stole my heart and made him the model for Lucky.

Acknowledgements

The author would like to thank the following for their help, which gave me added insight for this book:

Jennifer Reece's Grade 6 class from Glenrosa Elementary, who told me what a grandmother should be like, Karen Hansen, who gave me information about Agility Trials, Dr. Sheila McDonald, our veterinarian, who provided me with valuable information about euthanizing a pet, and Richie and Jeanne Cole, who introduced me to the working dogs of New Zealand.

1

I hate math!" I howled, blowing away the eraser crumbs for the umpteenth time. This percentage stuff was never going to make sense. It was totally useless! A ragged hole appeared in the centre of the page. "Oh no..." I moaned. Even though I disliked math, my notebook was always kept neat. Now it was an ugly mess. I threw the pencil down in disgust and tried to count to ten, which is supposed to help when you're really angry.

Usually, I loved sitting up here at the desk by the window in our den. It was my favourite thinking spot, but today it made me feel like a prisoner. Ever since my Grade Seven second term report card had come home some time ago, I'd had my nose in my books. There was just a little over a month before the end of the year to pull up my marks. It's not that I'm dumb or anything like that. It's just that there're so many other things to think about when you're in Grade Seven. The leaves on the tree outside my open window tossed about in the warm wind, calling me to hurry out. My mind began to drift into a daydream.

Suddenly a gust of wind leapt through the window, snatching at the pages of my open textbook and spilling a bag of potato chips across it. I scrambled to grab hold of everything, and in my haste knocked over a glass of grape juice that I'd just placed on the textbook to hold it open. Leaving a sticky purple trail, it galloped through the potato chips and across both books' pages. A few eraser crumbs floated along and disappeared with the juice as it dripped off the edge of my notebook.

"That does it!" I yelled to no one. Grabbing my notebook, I stuffed it between the pages of the textbook, juice, potato chips, eraser crumbs and all and squeezed it hard until I heard the chips crunch. Then, aiming at an old bird's nest in the tree, I pitched the whole thing through the open window. It struck a nearby branch and headed downward.

"What the heck!" my dad bellowed beneath. I held my breath, knowing what would come next. My smug satisfaction at getting rid of the math books evaporated. "NIKKI! Come down here... right now!"

A few moments later, I was standing in front of Dad, head bowed, hands behind my back.

Sometimes it's better to act contrite, even though you have the greatest urge to laugh. The scene was pretty funny, my dad standing under the tree, hands on his hips, with pages from my notebook fluttering about his feet, and the textbook sprawling a few feet away, a little crooked in the spine. My Sheltie dog, Wagner, crept from behind the tree where he'd been asleep and sat in front of Dad. He whined in sympathy.

"This just missed hitting me on the head. Nikki, don't you dare try and tell me these 'fell' out that window by accident!"

"No, they didn't fall out the window by accident. I threw them out! But..." I added, hoping to somewhat redeem myself, "...I was aiming at a bird's nest, not you."

"You...you threw them out?" For a moment he was speechless. He probably didn't expect an outright confession so quickly. Usually I work in a roundabout way, giving a few excuses first, so that by the time I actually confess, it sounds as if there was a good reason for my action. But today I was so angry that just didn't happen.

"Yes, I threw them out. I deplore math! I detest percentage, and I want nothing more to do with either of them!"

"Oh, I see," retorted my father, his face stiff with anger. He gestured towards the books. "How is *your teacher* going to feel about this?"

This was Dad's sick little joke. Whenever I had a problem with school, he said, "and how is your teacher going to feel about this?" It was enough to drive me nuts—the reason being—he WAS my teacher! Believe me, it's not the greatest, having your dad for your teacher.

"I don't care what my teacher feels about this," I said, stomping my foot and turning to leave.

"I suspect," my dad said evenly, although his face was still red, "that your teacher will be very angry if those math books show up in this condition on Monday morning without some good explanation, especially if the homework isn't done as well." He stepped around the books and headed for the house, Wagner at his side. Even my dog wasn't going to support me on this. Dad turned at the door. "I think your teacher will tell you that text book cost thirty dollars!"

My anger subsided as quickly as it had risen, and now the sight of my books made me feel a little sick. Why did my moods shift so quickly and so often? And why did I feel so strongly about things when they happened?

"Hormones," my mother would tell me. "You're at that age where your body is growing faster than your brains. Happens every year towards the end of Grade Six."

I guess she ought to know—she's a grade six teacher. Two teachers for parents! How much worse can it get? How helpful is it, though, knowing that your body is growing faster than your brains?

I thoughtfully picked up the books and cleaned them the best I could with outside tap water and the tail end of my T-shirt. Oh gosh, now there were purple stains on it too. I went down to my room to change and to count my babysitting money just in case "my teacher" was very angry on Monday regardless of my cleaning attempts.

2

Wagner opened one eye to acknowledge me as I stroked his silky back. He spent most of his time with me now that my cousin Trevor had moved out. Wagner had really gone for him when he'd come to stay with us last summer, maybe because Trevor seemed to need a friend and Wagner felt sorry for him. Dogs always seem to have compassion for people who need it. At the time, it had caused me to feel a little jealous, but now Wagner seemed like my dog again. I hugged him tightly, growling playfully at him, until his tail thumped the bed and he wriggled free, pouncing at me. Leaping off the bed, I grabbed my books and ran for the door.

"Come on, Wagner, let's go see Alisha. Maybe she knows how to do these dumb questions." We jogged down the road, Wagner bounding ahead of me and turning to bark at me every few steps.

Alisha's mom met me at the door. "Oh, hi Nikki, come on in." Wagner sat down, looking at her expectantly. "You too, Wagner. I think there may be a couple of doggy cookies left."

Following me in, Wagner sat politely on the rug by the door, wiggling in anticipation as his eyes followed Alisha's mom to the cupboard and back. This happened every time we came to Alisha's, so it didn't take any encouragement to get him to come with me.

"Alisha's gone to town with her dad to get Gran. They should be back soon." She held out the first biscuit to Wagner. He gently took it from her, crunched it once and swallowed. It always amazes me that dogs don't suffer indigestion when they do that.

He asked to be let out with the second one— the same as always. Sometimes he would run around the yard for a while before he stopped to eat it. I think he just enjoyed holding it in his mouth. Other times, he buried it. Today was a burying day. He wandered around the yard, stopping to sniff here and there before finding just the right spot at the edge of the flowerbed. Dirt flew in the air as he dug a small hole and dropped the dog biscuit in. With his nose he pushed the dirt back over it.

Alisha's mom laughed. "It's a good thing those don't sprout. We'd have doggy biscuits growing all over the yard!"

We heard a car coming up the road. "Oh, that will be them. I'd better put the kettle on for tea."

Alisha's grandmother was blonde and very pretty. She always dressed in beautiful clothes and wore the most delicious smelling perfume. While some people might have thought of me as a tomboy because I was quite often to be found riding my horse or reading up in the branches of my favourite tree, I also enjoyed getting dressed up once in a while and acting like a real lady. I would have loved to have a grandmother like Alisha's. To me she was the perfect lady! Besides that, she had a habit of buying Alisha expensive gifts. It was always exciting to see what new thing her grandmother brought her.

"Hi, Nikki," Alisha squealed when she saw me. She was wearing new running shoes that I'd have died for.

My parents didn't believe in buying expensive shoes for me, and it would take a lot of babysitting money to ever get such a pair. "Nice shoes!" I said.

"Thanks." Alisha tried to act nonchalant. "Gran bought them for me. She said my other ones were getting a bit scruffy."

A jealous pang nibbled at me. I hadn't seen my grandmother since I was just a little kid. I didn't ever remember receiving a gift from her. My feelings must have shown on my face.

"Come on," Alisha said, taking my arm, "let's grab some tea and cookies and go outside."

We filled two mugs with hot tea and added lots of honey while making small talk with Alisha's parents and her grandma. Alisha grabbed a stack of gingerbread cookies, and we headed for the door. I picked up my books on the way out.

Alisha frowned. "How come you brought those?"

"'Cause I can't figure out this stupid homework assignment on percentage. I've ruined my notebook." I let the books tumble to the ground as we sat down side by side on the garden swing.

Wagner followed us, his nose in the air. He would have been able to pick up the smell of gingerbread a mile away. As Alisha broke off a piece of her cookie for Wagner, she looked at the books lying open on the ground and started laughing.

"What a mess. You weren't kidding."

"Don't laugh. It's not funny!" My chin began to quiver.

Alisha put her arm around my shoulder. "What happened?"

She tried to keep a straight face as she listened to my story.

"Nikki, why don't you just ask your dad for help? He's our teacher, isn't he?" she finally asked.

I turned away from her. How could I explain? Somehow, the relationship I used to have with my dad had changed since the beginning of the school year. He didn't kid around with me as much or call me "Red" any more. Although that used to annoy me sometimes because I'm really not that keen on my hair colour, at the same time it made me feel kind of special.

There had been no choice about being in his classroom, because there was only one Grade Seven class at our school, and he was the teacher. So at the beginning of the school year, he'd told me the rules: no arguing, no talking back and I would have to be treated the same as everyone else in the class.

Somehow those rules seemed to affect everything at home too, and that's what drove me crazy. I usually have my own opinions about things, and it's hard not to be able to argue about them. Even before Dad was my teacher, I'd always disliked asking either of my parents for help with homework, because it usually ended up in an argument. I certainly wasn't going to ask now.

"Oh, all right," Alisha said to my silent back. "I can show you how to do those questions. Next time though, let's just do them together so you don't wreck any more books, okay?"

It didn't take very long for her to help me

figure out what I was doing wrong. I began to redo the assignment on a fresh page. I wasn't sure how I would do on a test, but for the moment it was making sense.

Alisha's mom appeared at the back door. "Oh, there you are. Shawn's here on his horse. He's looking for you, Nikki."

Shawn and his family had moved onto the acreage above us last year. He was in our Grade Seven class, and since he and I both owned horses, we enjoyed riding together. When he'd first moved into our neighbourhood, I'd had a crush on him, and so had Alisha for a while. Then we discovered he was more interested in horses than in boy-girl stuff, so all three of us just sort of hung out together.

Gathering up my books, we walked around to the front of the house where Shawn was standing in the driveway with Star beside him. Her head was down in the flowers bordering the driveway.

"Yikes, Star's eating the flowers. Get her out of there before Mom sees her," Alisha cried, waving her arms.

Shawn yanked on the reins, bringing Star's head up with an orange nasturtium dangling from her mouth. He gasped.

"Oh, sorry. I guess I was daydreaming," he said, grabbing the flower out of the horse's mouth and stuffing it under some nearby bushes. He stroked Star's neck. "Bad horse!" he scolded half-heartedly.

I laughed, "Mom puts nasturtiums in our salads sometimes. Star must have known that." I scratched behind her ear, and she bobbed her head in my direction.

"What's up?" I asked Shawn.

"I rode down to your house to see if you wanted to go for a ride, and your mom had just got home. They were reading a letter from your grandmother. She's coming for a visit or something." He frowned. "I didn't even know you had a grandmother. You've never mentioned her."

"My grandmother?" I was astonished. "She's lived in Australia for the last ten years. I don't even know her."

After my grandfather died, my dad's mom had remarried and moved to Australia. Dad hadn't thought much of her new husband, and there had been very little, if any, communication throughout the years. But now she was coming for a visit? Cool! Now Alisha wouldn't be the only one to have a grandma spoil her, one who dressed nicely and always looked good. Maybe she'd even buy me some shoes, just like Alisha's! It would be great to have a gran to call my own. All of this ran through my head in an instant, while Shawn and Alisha looked at me.

"Wow! I'd better go. I want to see when she's arriving. I'll phone you later, Shawn. Maybe we can go for a ride tonight. Thanks, Alisha," I called out breathlessly. "Come on Wagner," I shouted, but he was already far ahead of me. The excitement in my voice must have told him something special was happening at home.

*   *   *

The house was quiet. Mom and Dad were seated at the kitchen table, the one page letter lying open on the table between them.

"Shawn told me you got a letter from Grandma! He said she's coming for a visit. When is she arriving?" The words tumbled out before I realized that neither Mom nor Dad looked very happy. They glanced at each other as I slid into a chair and waited.

Dad ran his hands through his hair and sighed. "It sounds like she's arriving a week tomorrow."

"How long is she staying?" I looked from Dad to Mom and back again. "How come neither one of you seem very happy?"

Mom smiled. "We're not exactly unhappy. It's...it's just that, well, we weren't expecting to hear from her like this. It's a bit of a shock."

"What do you mean? What's the matter?" I asked, frowning.

Mom sighed. "Well, the fellow she was married to just died unexpectedly. She's broke, it seems, and has nowhere to go."

"You mean she's moving in with us for good?" I asked excitedly.

"Good heavens, I hope not!" Dad burst out. "Nikki, you don't know my mother! She's not your typical grandmother. She is very opinionated and has an extremely strong mind of her own. If she'd have listened to us years ago, she wouldn't be in such a fix now." Dad abruptly got up from the table and stalked towards the door. "Broke!" he muttered. "That's ridiculous!"

"Mom, please tell me what is going on. My only grandmother is coming for a visit, and I'm the only one excited. Has she got three heads or something?"

Mom laughed, covering my hand with hers for a moment. "It's not quite that bad. She is different, though. When your grandfather died, he left her very comfortable as far as money goes. On a trip to Australia the following year, she met a fellow she claimed to have fallen in love with. He had no money and no job—spent most of his time volunteering with environmental organizations.

In spite of our trying to talk some sense into her, she sold everything here and went to Australia to marry him. She's supported them all this time. It sounds like they spent all her money between them, no doubt trying to save the world." She rolled her eyes. "Now he's died. Don't get me wrong—I'm sorry to hear that—no one deserves to lose somebody they love."

Mom folded the letter up thoughtfully. "We'll have to clean the downstairs room Trevor used last summer." She tapped the letter against her chin. "Your dad and I both have a very busy month ahead of us at school. You'll have to help us entertain her, Nikki. It's going to be interesting, having her stay with us after so long."

"I don't care what's happened in the past. I think it's great she's coming," I said, getting up from the table. "I can hardly wait!"

3

Dear Diary,

I know I don't write to you often, only when I'm in a pensive mood, or when I'm extremely upset about something and writing about it seems to somehow help. My news today is very, very sad. It's terribly hard to write about it, although I know I must.

My dear, dear Wagner died last week, and I can hardly bear the pain of it. It's been the worst week of my entire life! I know I'll never get over losing him.

Wagner, as you know, was very afraid of thunderstorms. Sometimes he would frantically chase the sound of thunder, but usually he ran for the house and hid under the bed. We always tried to make sure he was inside when we expected a storm.

Last Sunday, we were away when a huge storm came up. We found him when we came home, all muddy and bedraggled by the side of the road. He seemed to be in terrible pain and couldn't get up, so Dad carried him to the house, where I wrapped him in my big bath towel. I prayed under my breath all the way to the vet's while Wagner whined softly, his eyes pleading with me to stop his hurting.

After examining him, the vet said his back was broken from being struck by a car and there was nothing she could do to save him. He would have to be euthanized.

Now comes the hard part, Dear Diary, because she asked me if I wanted to be with him until the end. Dad, who was almost as emotional as I was at that point, didn't think it was a good idea, but how could I leave my dear, dear friend to die by himself?

I held him in my arms as she gave him a shot of painkiller to dull his senses. A few minutes later, she gave him the final shot. Then she went out of the room and left us alone. Soon after, he gave a little shudder and lay limply in my arms. It was the hardest thing I've ever done, but I'm glad I did it.

When we got home, I laid Wagner on the grass and brushed the mud out of his coat until it shone again. Then I buried my face in his fur one last time and wept.

That evening we buried Wagner by a maple tree

in Ginger's pasture. Alisha picked some flowers from her mom's garden, and Shawn made a white cross for the grave on which he had painted:

Here lies Wagner: the best Sheltie ever
May he rest in Peace.

Dad, Mom, Alisha, Shawn and I took turns telling the story we best remembered about Wagner. My story was about the time that Alisha and I had camped out in our yard in my pup tent. Wagner had got so excited on top of the air mattresses that he'd caused the tent to collapse on all of us.

Oh, Dear Diary, it's been almost a week and the hollow ache in my stomach just won't go away. I don't feel like eating or doing much else. Mom and Dad say that it's time to move on now, and to think about maybe getting a new dog.

I could never replace Wagner! I just keep thinking about the feel of his warm body when he'd snuggle up against me at night, the way his wet nose would poke against me whenever he wanted my attention, and his playful bark when he saw the Frisbee in my hand. Worst of all, I can picture his liquid golden eyes that always seemed to know exactly what I was thinking. Losing a pet must be the most terrible thing a kid can ever experience.

It's funny how things you're terribly excited

about one day can suddenly hold no interest. Last week I could hardly wait for my grandmother's arrival tomorrow. Now I just don't care.

P.S.: Dear Diary,
I never, ever want to own another dog! I can't bear the thought of such a loss again!

4

The doorbell rang a few times before I could summon the interest to answer it. Mom and Dad had gone to town for groceries, anticipating my grandmother's arrival that night by plane. They'd asked me if I wanted to go with them, but I had a math test to study for and besides, I just didn't feel like being around people.

I glanced out the window to see a wiry little woman with a very full pack on her back and a bulging old canvas bag under her arm. Her back towards the door, she stood shading her eyes with her free hand, watching some birds in a nearby tree. Strange! No one had ever arrived on our doorstep with a backpack. She must be lost, I thought.

I opened the door a few inches, leaving the lock on the screen.

"Yes?" I asked.

She turned towards the door, squinting in at me.

"You must be Nikki."

I opened the door a little wider. "Who are you?" I asked a bit stupidly.

Pulling off a cotton hat, she smacked it against her leg, sending a puff of dust into the air. Piercing blue eyes met mine through wire-rimmed glasses that had seen better days. "Well, supposing that you are Nikki, I guess I'm your Grandmother Iris."

I stared at her, this shapeless person in a man's plaid shirt, well-worn jeans tucked into scruffy leather hiking boots...a sun-etched face that wasn't used to smiling, cropped, straight, mousy grey hair. She couldn't possibly be my grandmother!

She shifted the pack from one hip to the other. "Look, girl...I can't stand here all day. I'm tired from walking up that hill! This wretched pack is heavy. Are you going to invite me in or not?"

Speechless, I unlatched the screen door and held it for her as she bumped past me, dropping the canvas bag onto the floor.

"Whew!" she whistled. "I'd forgotten how steep that hill is." Wincing, she eased the pack off her shoulders onto the floor, then shrugged her shoulders a few times and stretched. She looked around the room.

"Where are your parents?"

I realized I'd been holding my breath watching her. "They're...they're in town getting groceries. They thought you'd be flying in tonight from Vancouver."

"Had my fill of those gas-guzzling jets on my trip from Australia. Caught the bus this morning."

I chewed my lip. "They should be back soon."

She wandered over to the sliding glass doors to look at the view for a moment, then turned and meandered around the living room, hands on her hips.

"I see they're still into consumerism!" she muttered.

"Into what?" I asked, confused.

She swung around to face me. "Consumerism— buying stuff—buying stuff you don't really need. Squandering the earth's resources!"

Frowning, I looked around the living room. What was she talking about? The new furniture my parents had bought this past spring? She hadn't seen my parents in ten years. What right did she have to criticize them! A little voice inside me whined, "And what right does she have as my grandmother to look like a scruffy little homeless person?"

All of this ran through my head as I tried to figure out what to say in response. Fortunately, my parents arrived at that moment, just before I said something I would no doubt have later regretted.

Mom and Dad seemed a bit reserved in their greetings; I could understand why. They also seemed a bit embarrassed that they hadn't been there when she arrived.

"I should have known you'd pull a trick like catching the bus and then another bus and then trekking up the hill with all your belongings! Why didn't you call us?" Dad asked her, half scolding.

"What good would it have done? You weren't home anyway. Besides, why have you come and get me when I could catch the bus. It would just be an unnecessary trip," Grandmother retorted, her chin in the air.

Dad smiled ruefully. "Well, I see you haven't changed."

"No, and don't expect me to, either!" she answered.

Mom kept blowing wisps of hair out of her eyes as she and I unpacked the groceries. She does this when she's stressed out. Dad took my grandmother down to show her her room.

Soon we were collected around the dining room table having a bowl of soup that Mom had hastily taken out of the freezer. Usually, our dinner table is fairly alive with conversation.

Mom and Dad try to compete with each other about how their day has been, and on Sundays it's just general stuff about what's been going on with me and in the neighbourhood. Not this Sunday, though.

I still didn't have much of an appetite. "Nikki, eat your soup and don't slurp it," from my mother. "Is your homework done? Don't forget you have a test tomorrow!" from my father. That was about it for dinner conversation. That and a bit of small talk directed towards my grandmother. "How was your flight? What time did you get in? How was your bus trip from Vancouver?"

It struck me as very strange that no one asked the big questions, such as: "What have you been doing these past ten years?", "What are your plans?" and the big one that probably weighed the most on everyone's mind: "How long are you planning on staying?"

I excused myself as soon as possible on the pretense that I needed to study. For the rest of the evening I stayed in my room. For a while I honestly did try to study. Then I tried to read. Finally, I put my pjs on and turned the lights out. My hands ran over the empty spot on the bed, and before I knew it, tears began to trickle down my face again. It took me a few minutes to realize that I was weeping not only for Wagner now, but for myself as well. A week ago, I'd been so excited about my grandmother's arrival. The person who'd arrived was about as far from the type of grandmother I'd expected as could be.

A while later I heard a sound like quiet sobbing coming from the room next to mine. I placed my ear against the wall to listen better. It couldn't be my grandmother. Not the antagonistic, self-assured person I'd met today. I climbed back into bed. Pulling the blankets up tight under my chin, I lay there thoughtfully and listened some more. It had to be her. It's funny, but I didn't feel any sympathy for her. Rather, I found myself hoping she wouldn't be staying long.

5

Ten minutes before my alarm was due to go off the next morning, I awoke feeling groggy and grumpy. Usually, I kind of enjoy waking up so early, so I can lie there for a few minutes listening to the birds outside my window before getting up to do my chores. When I come back from Ginger's barn, the sun is usually just bursting over the mountains, spilling its rosy light onto the lake in the valley below. Sometimes I get so involved watching the sun rise that I'm almost late for school!

That morning, though, instead of birds, I heard a rhythmic noise outside. Whack...whack... whack! That's what must have awakened me. Irritated that I was missing ten minutes of precious sleep, I crawled out of bed and went to the window to investigate.

It was my grandmother hacking at weeds in a plot of dirt near the house. Her face showed no sign of the sorrow I'd heard late last night, but it didn't display happiness either. Instead, she looked a bit disgusted at the task she was attempting.

I quickly threw my clothes on. Rather than going out the basement door where I would meet her, I went upstairs and out the front door. I ran through the pasture grass, thick morning dew grabbing at my ankles, and tried not to look at Wagner's grave. Ginger whinnied softly to me, bobbing her head to say that she was ready to be let out.

"We'll try to go for a ride tonight, okay?" I said, scratching her nose while I undid the paddock gate to let her into her pasture. Grabbing the pitchfork, I cleaned out her barn. Lastly, I turned the hose on to fill her water trough.

By the time I got back to the house, Mom and Dad were at the table eating breakfast. Grandmother was still outside hoeing.

"What's she doing that for?" I asked, watching her through the window as I poured cereal into a bowl.

Dad shrugged his shoulders. "Beats me...but I know better than to ask."

"She probably thinks we need a vegetable garden," Mom said.

"And she's going to grow one in that clay soil? It's hard as a rock. Good luck!" Dad muttered.

Suddenly, Mom and Dad both put down their coffee cups and just looked at each other. It came to all of us at the same time. A garden took all spring, summer and into fall to grow.

"Does that mean she'll be here until fall?" I asked in disbelief.

Dad cleared his voice, still looking at Mom. "Well, we're not quite sure."

I felt even more glum. "Why is she up so early? Doesn't she eat breakfast?"

Dad got up from the table. "All in her own good time. Like I told you before, my mother has a mind of her own. She pretty much marches to her own drummer."

Looking at the clock, Mom got up too. "We're going to be late if we don't get going. I'll put out a place setting for her, and we'll leave the cereal..."

"She'll be fine," Dad muttered as he grabbed his lunch and headed for the door, Mom following him. I watched as they talked with my grandmother for a moment. Dad gestured at the work she'd been doing, shaking his head. Grandmother threw her arms about a bit, then leaned on the hoe, nodding her head and smiling smugly. It was pretty clear she wasn't about to give up on her idea, in spite of my dad probably telling her it was hopeless. With a short wave,

Mom and Dad left for work.

I quickly put my dishes into the dishwasher, made myself a peanut butter sandwich and ran downstairs for my books. Once again I came back upstairs so I could leave by the front door. I couldn't think of anything I wanted to say to my grandmother.

Usually, I meet Alisha, and we walk to school together. Sometimes, Shawn joins us. Today, I was a bit late and missed both of them, arriving at school just before the bell.

"What's she like?" Alisha whispered as my father read the morning announcements and started talking about the math test.

"Who?" I whispered back, knowing very well whom she meant.

"Your grandmother, silly!" Alisha whispered.

"Oh her, she's..."

"NIKKI, don't talk when I'm talking. You know the rules of our classroom," my father's voice boomed.

Alisha looked out the window as if she had been minding her own business. Everyone else looked at me.

"Take one test and three sheets of foolscap and pass the rest back," Dad instructed the front person in each row. "Remember, you have forty minutes to complete the test. Talking during it will result in a score of zero."

We all settled down to concentrate. Alisha had done a good job helping me. I was pretty sure I would do really well. I began to enjoy the challenge. After I finished each question, I checked it over to make sure I'd done it correctly.

When I was nearly done, I glanced at the clock. If I hurried, I would get to read my library book for a few minutes. I quickly wrote my name and the date at the top of the last page of foolscap, and then, being a neat freak, I proceeded to draw a ruler line along the top margin to set it apart from my work. In my haste, I pushed too hard.

SNAP! The lead on my pencil broke off at the base. I looked up at the clock again—I had only five minutes left to do two questions and check them.

"Psst...Alisha, loan me a pencil, will you?" I whispered quietly.

Within seconds it seemed, Dad was standing beside my desk, glowering at me.

"Nikki, you know the rules," he said in a quiet, even voice. "Your test will have to be destroyed."

"But my pencil broke! I was just trying to borrow one from Alisha," I said in disbelief.

"I'm sorry," he said in a voice that to me didn't sound sorry at all, "but I just explained the rule about not talking during the test." He sighed.

"You knew what the consequence of breaking that rule would be…" He put his hand out for the test.

"Fine!" I shouted. Grabbing the test sheets and crumpling them into a tight ball, I dropped it on the desk. If he wanted it, he was going to have to pick it up and throw it in the garbage himself. I slouched down in my seat, my arms across my chest, and stared past him out the window. The classroom was deathly silent.

Without another word, he picked up the ball of crumpled paper, turned on his heel and went back to his desk. Curtly, he gave directions for the collection of the rest of the tests, gathered some books together and left the room to teach music to the Grade Fives.

I leapt to my feet and ran for the cloakroom door before Miss Willis, our gym teacher, came to collect our class. My face felt hot, and I knew that everyone was whispering. I just couldn't face any of them right now.

I set out on the walk home, unsure of where else to go. With each step, I relived the unfairness and humiliation of what had happened. Trudging up the hill, I brushed away tears that kept pooling in my eyes and trickling down my face. Mom, of course, was at her school, but, as I walked up the driveway, I remembered my grandmother.

The little plot of ground she'd been working on had been dug up and turned over, but she was nowhere to be seen. I snuck in the basement door and went directly to my room, where I threw myself into a miserable heap on the bed and closed my eyes.

"You sick?"

Grandmother stood at the door. She was wearing the same shirt and jeans as yesterday, only now they were both grimy from her gardening. Her hair was plastered to her head from wearing her hat.

"No," I said, rolling over to face the wall.

"How come you're home then?"

I didn't need any more people telling me what I'd done was wrong. "'Cause I'm mad," I said, hoping that would satisfy her enough so she'd leave.

"What about?" she asked.

I rolled back over to look at her. "Dad threw away my math test because I was talking during a test. It means I'll get zero on the test!"

She continued leaning against the door frame with her arms folded across her chest, watching me. I sat up.

"That's not why I'm mad, though. It wasn't like I was cheating. I knew all the material. I'm pretty sure all my answers were right! My pencil broke, and I just had a couple of minutes to finish two questions, so I asked Alisha for another pencil. That's when he caught me." I stood up, scowling at her. "You probably think he's right."

"Doesn't matter what I think, girl. It's what you think that counts. Did you stand up for what you believed was right?"

I swallowed hard. This wasn't the reaction I'd expected.

"Yes, sort of..."

"No, you didn't. You ran away from it. If I were you, I'd go back to try to work things out."

"But you don't know my dad," I spluttered.

She put her hands on her hips. "Well, I ought to... He's my son, isn't he?"

We glared at each other. Then she seemed to relent a little. "It's been so long since I've been around him—maybe you do know him better than I do." She sniffed. "He always was pigheaded. Don't imagine that's changed."

"Pigheaded? What do you mean?" I asked a little crossly.

"Well, he certainly has a mind of his own. Whatever he thinks, he thinks is right!"

I almost smiled. That's exactly what Dad had said about her. But I didn't know her well enough to know if she'd see any humour in it.

We were both silent, lost in our own thoughts.

I didn't want to talk about Dad any more. I was going to have to figure out what to do about that on my own.

"I'm sorry about your husband," I blurted out to change the subject.

Grandmother looked at me without speaking.

"I...I heard you crying last night. It must be hard for you. What was he like?" I asked, suddenly realizing that I really did want to know.

Grandmother walked over to the window, her back to me. "He was a good person...no matter what you've been told." She paused for a moment. "I heard you crying last night as well."

I hadn't expected to share the news about Wagner's death with my grandmother. I didn't need any sympathy, nor did I expect any from her.

"My dog died last week, that's all," I said.

Grandmother turned towards the door. "I guess we've both lost someone who meant a lot to us." She cleared her throat. "You going back to school?"

"Yeah, I guess so," I said, following her outside. I didn't add that I wasn't planning on speaking to my dad about the test. I'd cooled off a little and decided that the best plan was to ignore him for the rest of the day. I was pretty sure Grandmother would say I was still "running away", but I didn't care what she thought anyway.

6

"S o what's she like?" Alisha asked as the three of us walked home after school. Alisha and Shawn had so far avoided comment on what had happened between Dad and me, for which I was grateful. When I'd arrived back at school, everyone had acted like I'd never left. I was back before gym was over, so Dad never knew I'd left either. The whole thing seemed like a bad dream.

"Who?" I asked, pretending for the second time that I didn't know whom she meant. Shawn walked ahead of us, whacking at dandelions along the side of the road with a stick he'd picked up.

Alisha rolled her eyes. "Your grandmother!"

"She's okay, I guess... She's different, that's for sure."

Shawn stopped whacking the dandelions and waited for us to catch up.

"What do you mean, 'different'?" he asked.

"Well..." I replied thoughtfully, "she's... 'earthy'. She arrived with a backpack on her back and an old canvas bag. That must be everything she owns, although I just can't imagine it."

"Cool!" Shawn exclaimed. "She sounds great!" He took off again, walking ahead of us. I frowned.

"What did she bring you?" Alisha asked.

I looked down at her new shoes. I just couldn't admit my grandmother had brought me nothing, even though I couldn't imagine what I'd have wanted out of that old backpack anyway.

"A book," I blurted out. "She brought me a beautiful book."

"What kind of book?" Alisha asked.

"Oh, it's..."

"Come here, you guys. Look at this!" Shawn called, interrupting the next lie I was about to weave.

He was pointing with his stick to a nest in the low bough of a fir tree next to the ditch.

"I just saw a robin fly out. I bet she has eggs in there." He jumped across the ditch and pushed another bough out of the way so we could look in.

"Oh, be careful," I whispered. I loved bird's eggs and baby birds. I didn't want Shawn's clumsy efforts hurting anything that might be there.

"I will. Don't worry. Look!"

We all peered in at the four sky blue robin's eggs that were nestled together in the downy nest.

"Don't touch them," I warned, "or the mother

may not come back."

"There she is." He pointed his stick towards the top of the fir tree, where the mother robin swayed in the wind, watching us. Shawn gently let the bough go. We scrambled back across the ditch onto the road. It was going to be fun waiting for the baby birds to hatch.

We said goodbye to Alisha at her driveway and walked in companionable silence towards my house. Fortunately, she hadn't asked again about the book my grandmother was supposed to have given me. I hoped she'd forget it. Why did I say that? I thought angrily.

"Nikki...about your test this morning..." Shawn said.

I turned away. "I don't want to talk about it!"

"Yeah, I didn't think you would." He kicked at the dirt on the road. "I...I just want you to know that I don't think what happened was fair to you."

"Thanks," I mumbled as I turned into our driveway.

"We never went for our ride last night," he called out. "Do you want to go tonight?"

"Sure," I called back. "Phone me after dinner, okay?" I hadn't looked forward to being around my father tonight. Now I had the perfect excuse not to be.

Grandmother was in the garage. My mountain bike stood upside down in front of her. After squirting oil around the chain, she spun the tire, bending down eye level with the wheel.

"This yours?" she asked when she saw me standing in the doorway.

"Yeah, it's my old bike. I don't use it any more. I need a new one."

She straightened up. "Nonsense," she said. "What's wrong with this one?"

"It's old and heavy. Besides, it's only got eighteen gears. I want one with twenty-four gears. I'm hoping to get a new mountain bike for my birthday this weekend."

Grandmother snorted in disgust.

"Mind if I use it?" she asked, clumsily tipping it back onto its wheels.

"What for?"

She squinted at me, ready to gauge my reaction to what she was going to say.

"To ride to town for garden seeds."

The idea of my grandmother riding into town, then back up our hill was beyond me. The hill alone tired me out, and I'd never ridden as far as town, which was a long way. She really was loony!

I shrugged. "I don't care, but my helmet is broken. It's against the law here to ride without a helmet."

She glanced around the garage as if checking to make sure I was telling the truth.

"Mom should be home shortly. She'd probably drive you in," I said.

"I can't have a car driving to town just for that," she muttered.

I shrugged my shoulders. If she wanted to be that silly, it was her problem. At that moment, Mom drove in. She looked at Grandmother, the bike and me, but didn't ask any questions.

"I have to go to town for a few things. Thought you might like to go," she said, looking at Grandmother.

"I do at that," Grandmother said, climbing in.

"I'm coming too," I said, opening the back door. Normally, that's the last thing I would have done, but I didn't particularly want to be home when Dad arrived.

"So, how was your day, Nikki?" Mom asked as we drove towards town.

"Mmm..." I replied.

"How did your math test go?"

I should have known that would be the next question. Grandmother started whistling "Waltzing Matilda". She rolled down her window so that wind swept in and further tousled her untidy hair. Maybe she figured I'd lie, and she didn't want to hear it. But I'd lied enough today. I could see Mom watching me in her rear view mirror, waiting for an answer.

"I hate being in Dad's class!" I exploded. "He's so unfair! Can't I transfer into town, or something?"

"Whatever happened?" She continued glancing at me in her mirror, concern etched on her face.

"Kay, for Heaven's sake, watch where you're driving," Grandmother scolded.

Mom's eyes shifted back to the road. "I guess you'll have to tell me about this later..."

I nodded dumbly.

"FOR SALE: HUBCAPS AND PUPPIES," Grandmother read aloud as we approached two signs, one above the other, in front of an unsightly yard that was full of silver hubcaps. They were mounted in tall rows on anything and everything available, even on trees. The sun caught them and made the reflection so bright I had to close my eyes.

Grandmother "tsk-tsked". "Just think," she said, "of all those fancy gas guzzling cars being driven too fast and losing their hubcaps."

"Speaking of that very thing, I lost one recently," Mom said, slowing down and putting on her turn signal. "I wonder if he's got one like mine."

Grandmother groaned as Mom turned into the yard. "I'll stay here," she said.

"Me too," I said as Mom got out. I hadn't really wanted to come. I felt miserable and a little bit argumentative.

Scowling, I stared at the back of Grandmother's head. "How come you hate cars so much?" I asked.

She shook her head. "'Cause they're ruining the environment! When you have Inuit hunters falling through the ice they've always hunted on because of global warming, it's time we changed our way of thinking! I bet there are five times as many cars here now as when I lived here. How many do you think will be here by the time you grow up?"

"I don't know," I answered truthfully. "Didn't you have a car in Australia?"

"Nope! Wouldn't own one! Got around just fine using bikes and these!" She slapped her legs. "We used the bus or train if we had to go a distance." I silently tried to imagine life without two cars in the garage. It was impossible.

Grandmother looked out the window. "At least he's selling one good thing." Her voice softened. "Look at the puppies."

Under a scraggly fir tree was a makeshift enclosure made of chicken wire and an old sheet of plywood. Three puppies wandered around inside, but from this distance it was impossible to tell how old they were or what kind they were.

I really didn't care.

"Maybe that's what you need..."

"No!" I blurted out. "I don't want another dog!"

Grandmother shrugged her shoulders and was silent.

I hadn't really meant to shout at her. "It's...it's just that I don't ever want to go through losing another dog," I said.

Grandmother nodded. "I know what you mean."

"Have you ever had a dog?" I asked as Mom approached the car empty-handed.

She nodded again. "I've had a lot of good dogs in my lifetime. Losing them never did get any easier."

"He doesn't have a hubcap that matches, at least not now," Mom said getting into the car. "He says he gets more each week." I smiled to myself as Grandmother groaned again.

I leaned back and let the warm wind play over my face. Sometime I would ask Grandmother about the dogs she had owned. I suddenly realized there were a few other things I'd like to ask her about too.

7

I jogged along on Ginger behind Shawn as we started up the trail to Watson's Pond, one of our favourite destinations. It was a ten-minute ride from our house, and it was such an interesting place to visit. Last fall we'd discovered a group of turtles living there. It was always fun to see what they were doing. We'd named each one, but we were clever enough to realize that they probably didn't know their names!

The trail at the beginning was only wide enough for one horse. Ginger didn't think much of having to follow rather than lead as she usually did. She kept trying to get close enough to Star so that she could rush past her at the first opportunity. Tightening the reins, I scolded her gently. She bobbed her head, her ears flickering as if to listen, but I knew she was watching for the trail to widen.

I missed Wagner running along beside us, crashing in and out of the bush, nosing after squirrels and quail. I swallowed quickly and took several deep breaths of the wild, late spring air.

Ginger's muscles began to quiver in anticipation. I allowed her to come up alongside Star, then I pulled her into a walk.

Shawn glanced over at me. "Your grandmother's kind of cool!" he said.

I wrinkled my nose. "What makes you think that?"

"I was talking to her while she was planting the garden. She told me she liked my mode of transportation."

I laughed. "Yeah, I bet she did! She doesn't like cars."

"I know. She told me about your trip to the hubcap yard."

"She told you all that? She hasn't spoken that much to me since she arrived."

Shawn looked at me sideways. "You don't seem to like her much."

I shrugged. "I don't really know her. She's not what I expected. She certainly is opinionated."

Shawn laughed. "The two of you should get along well. At least she's not like old lady Harrison. One of these days she's going to break her neck wobbling around on her high heels!"

I gasped. "If Alisha heard you talking about her grandmother like that, she'd be mad."

"Well, it's true. At least your grandmother dresses sensibly." He leaned down low over Star's neck and loosened the reins. "I'll race you to the pond," he yelled.

Star leapt forward, but Ginger had already sensed the challenge and charged ahead of her. She stretched out beneath me, her hooves pounding the ground rhythmically, her mane flying up to mingle with my hair. Ginger loved to run. Tonight, the scent of spring in the air seemed to act like a tonic on her. Shades of green and the warm evening wind rushed past us as we seemed almost to fly over the ground.

Shawn and I had learned from experience to use the large birch a couple of hundred meters back from the pond as our finishing line. That way we had time to slow the horses down and stop them before we actually got to the pond. We seemed to reach the birch tree all too soon. Reluctantly, I pulled up on the reins.

"Whoa, whoa," I coaxed Ginger gently until she slowed to a trot, then a prance and finally a walk. I patted her neck as she chomped on her bit. "Good girl," I crooned. She had broken into a sweat, so I turned and walked her back to meet Shawn, who was just passing the birch.

We tied the horses loosely to a tree and sat down on a log.

"That was awesome!" I said, pulling my hair back off my face.

Shawn looked at me. "Your eyes are all sparkly," he said. He picked up a pebble and tossed it into the pond where it made a hollow plunking noise before it sank into the depths.

"So are yours," I said, glancing at his face. Shyness overtook both of us for a moment.

"Your hair's a mess, though," he said, laughing.

"So is yours," I said, pushing him off the log so that he sprawled onto the damp grass. He rolled over and sat up, still chuckling. "Now look what you've done. I have grass stains on my new jeans."

"Serves you right," I retorted. With a sigh, I leaned back against a tree trunk and closed my eyes to listen. I like doing this because you hear lots of things you wouldn't if your eyes were open: the soft blowing of the horses, the clinking of the bits in their mouths, the squeak of the saddle's leather as they moved around eating, young tree leaves tapping in the breeze, a mallard's wings beating the air as he came quacking in to make a landing on the pond. Somewhere near my left ear, a mosquito's whining drone came nearer and nearer. I opened my eyes and shooed it away.

Shawn was standing at the edge of the pond. "Look, the turtles," he called, pointing to the other side of the pond. We made our way through the bushes and tall grass towards them. We stopped at a clump of cattails, where the swampy water would come over the tops of our shoes if we tried to go further. From there we could see five turtles lined up on a floating log. From observing them other days, I knew they would soon all plop into the water and disappear for the night.

"There's Alice," I said, pointing to the biggest one. She always seemed to maintain the best spot on the log. I secretly admired her for being the boss.

"You mean Alex!" Shawn teased. "He looks pretty macho to me." We always had this little debate about whether this large dominant turtle was a male or female, and since neither of us had ever handled the turtles and probably wouldn't know how to tell the difference anyhow, we just continued to tease each other about it.

"No way. It's Alice, and those are her last year's babies: Janet, Myrtle, Sabrina and Timmy." We watched as the large turtle slid into the water and gracefully sank out of sight. The others followed. "See, she's putting them to bed," I said smugly.

Shawn chuckled. "Yeah, right! That's Alex, I tell you. He's the father, and he's probably taking them out for pizza and a baseball game."

"Pizza and a baseball game on the bottom of the pond," I said laughing. "I like that! I'm going to use it for my next story in creative writing." Turning away from the pond, something red in the bushes caught my eye.

We pushed our way up the bank and through the bulrushes and thick scrub until we came to a large spot where the underbrush had been flattened. A length of red plastic tape fluttered from the low branch of a pine.

"Surveyor's tape," Shawn said. "I wonder what they're doing in here. Look, there's a pin." He pointed to a metal stake that had been pounded into the ground.

I bent down to look at the pin but could see nothing on it that gave any clue as to why it was there.

"What's that for?"

Shawn shrugged. "I think it means somebody's marking the boundary of their land."

The idea of some person actually owning land in the pond area had never occurred to me. It was just a wild, beautiful spot that seemed to belong to the birds and the turtles. Surely that could never change.

"I wonder where the other pins are," Shawn muttered, shading his eyes against the setting sun and scanning every direction as far as he could see.

"I don't know, but we'd better head for home now. Let's come back this weekend. Since Saturday's my birthday, let's ride over on Sunday," I said, leading the way back to the horses. I didn't really see the need in looking for pins in the ground but would gladly ride over to the pond any time for any reason.

"Are you having a party?" Shawn asked.

I'd already given some thought to that. I didn't really want a bunch of kids over when I had such a strange grandmother living with me. I wasn't into big parties anyway.

"Yeah, a pizza party. You and Alisha are invited," I said, untying Ginger and climbing up onto her back.

Shawn grinned. "A pizza party...just like the turtles."

I grinned back. "Yeah, just like the turtles, only we'll watch videos instead of playing baseball."

By the time we got back and I had unsaddled Ginger and brushed her down, it was almost dark. Dad was sitting at the kitchen table reading. He looked up as I came in.

"Nikki, I think we need to talk," he said, closing the newspaper and deliberately folding it up. I sank into the chair opposite him. I'd been dreading this moment since I'd come home from school.

"I realize you think that what happened today was unfair to you." He glanced at me. "I want you to know that I realize you weren't cheating. I know you wouldn't do that."

"Then why did you say my paper had to be destroyed?" I demanded, feeling my anger returning.

Dad ran his hands through his hair and sighed. "Try to look at it from my perspective. I had just told the entire class that there was to be no talking during the test. I also described the consequence of talking. What sort of treatment do you suppose another student would expect if they did the same thing after I'd made an exception to that rule for you?"

I shrugged. "I guess they'd expect to be treated the same. If they were only asking to borrow another pencil, like I was, then it wouldn't be fair to them either!"

"Yes, but that might not always be the truth. They might in fact be cheating. I don't want to have to be a judge, Nikki. I just want to be a teacher." He smiled. "If the police stopped me for speeding through our school zone, how sympathetic do you think they'd be if I told them I was going home for lunch, and I was late?"

"Oh, Dad! Now you're being silly," I said, trying to hold back a smile. I was beginning to see his point, and while I still felt a bit bitter about the whole thing, I promised myself to be well-prepared during the next test. I would have lots of erasers and sharpened pencils ready.

"Anyway, 'Red', you'll be happy to know I couldn't resist looking at your paper. I wanted to see if Alisha was a good teacher." He smiled. "She must know what she's doing. Your answers were all right!"

"You mean I got 100% on my test, and I won't get an 'A' on my report card?" I moaned.

He leaned back in his chair, eyeing me thoughtfully for a moment. "I think you've probably learned a lesson today that counts for a great deal. You've also been working hard to learn about percentage, and that effort counts for a lot. What happened won't reflect negatively on your report card. Besides," he added with a twinkle in his eye, "I wouldn't want to have to face your other parent and try to defend myself in a parent/teacher interview!"

A wave of relief swept over me. I jumped up and hugged him.

"I guess it's not easy having your dad as your teacher, is it?" he asked.

"It hasn't been that much fun," I said

thoughtfully, "but I'm starting to realize that it's been hard on you too." I kissed him on the cheek. "I'm tired. I think I'll go to bed. Good night."

"Oh, Nikki," Dad asked as I reached the door, "is your homework done?"

My homework! Oh, my gosh! I smiled and blew him another kiss. "It's just about to be!" I left him, shaking his head and laughing.

8

"A home made pizza! I've never heard of such a thing," I protested.

Grandmother threw a sideways glance at Mom, who was humming a tune as she cleaned out the cutlery drawer. "I don't doubt that! It's time you learned to cook, girl."

Mom stopped humming. "Nikki makes good salads," she interjected half-heartedly.

"Salads are fine, but I mean real cooking." Grandma frowned. "You're going to be thirteen tomorrow. It's high time you learned how to make a meal. Tell you what. I'll help you make pizza tomorrow if you'll help me build a chicken house this afternoon."

The spoons Mom had just lifted clattered back into the drawer. Our eyes met and we chorused together, "A chicken house!"

"But we don't have any chickens," I protested.

"We will have by Monday. I ordered a dozen chicks today."

"I was afraid you'd say something like that," Mom said.

"Beats me," Grandmother went on, "how anyone can own an acreage and not raise their own chickens to provide them with eggs and meat."

Mom and I looked at each other. I'm sure we were thinking the same thing: How long does it take a chicken to grow up? About the same amount of time as for a garden to grow, I decided. It looked like Grandma was firmly entrenched in our household at least until fall.

I had to admit the neat mounded rows of soil with stakes at either end looked a lot better than the patch of weeds that had always been there. Even Dad seemed impressed. I was eager to see who was right. Dad didn't think the soil would grow anything, and Grandma obviously thought it would.

Mom blew a wisp of hair out of her eyes. "I think your idea of making a pizza is good. Write a list of what you'll need, and I'll run to town for it."

Grandma's eyes lit up. "Was hoping you'd say that. While you're there, will you pick up some inch-and-a-half nails? Found a hammer and saw and some scrap lumber, but no nails."

"Oh, Iris, you are unbelievable!" Mom said, smiling. Then she started laughing. It was the first time I'd heard her really laugh since

Grandmother had arrived. "Yes, I'll get everything you need. Write it all down. I'll get my purse."

Just as Mom was about to leave, Dad came in. "Where are you off to? What's happening?" he asked, looking at all three of us.

Mom raised her eyebrows and looked at him knowingly, which was the same as telling him not to ask any more questions, just to do as she asked. "I'm off to town for some things. Come with me for the drive."

"Okay, whatever you say." Shrugging his shoulders, Dad followed her out the door.

Before they got back, Grandma and I had hauled pieces of old plywood and two-by-fours out to where she planned on adding the chicken house onto the side of an old shed. Then she taught me how to cut the plywood in a straight line by kneeling on it to hold it steady and keeping my eye over top of the blade. I was just cutting the third piece to her specifications when Dad appeared with the bag of nails.

"So, I hear we're getting chickens," he said with a small smile.

"You've got the room for them, and I've got the time," Grandma replied without looking up from where she was measuring and marking a two-by-four.

"Hmm," was all Dad said. He wandered over to

watch me as I kneeled on the fourth piece of plywood and began sawing. Without saying anything, he steadied the side while I laboriously sawed down the pencil line I'd drawn along the length of it with the square. Then he stepped back and watched for a few more minutes as Grandma cut then nailed the two-by-fours against the side of the old shed. As we lifted the first piece of plywood into place, I noticed he was gone.

By dinnertime, we had the little house completed. I stepped back to look at our handiwork. A couple of years ago, it would have been great to have a playhouse like this. It wasn't fancy, but I could imagine it would be a pretty good home for twelve little chicks. It was amazing that Grandma knew how to build something like that. Now I knew as well.

"You have to see our chicken house, Mom," I said through a mouthful of stir-fry at the dinner table. "I can hardly wait to see those cute, fluffy little chicks running around inside it."

Grandma frowned. "Hold on, Nikki. They're going to be more like scrawny half-grown chickens than bits of fluff."

I wrinkled my nose. "Yuck! How come?"

"Because it's the middle of June. I want to be eating some of those chickens by fall. Pass the bread, please," Grandmother said matter of factly.

I put down my fork. "How will they be killed?" I asked slowly.

"Someone will chop off their heads. Probably me..." Grandma looked up from her plate at each one of us. "Unless one of you wants to do it."

"Gross! That's disgusting," I cried. "We just finished building a nice home for them, and you're already planning their deaths by chopping their heads off!"

Grandma looked at me, surprised. "We didn't build that house out of the goodness of our hearts for homeless chickens, you know." She scooped up a forkful of chicken from her stir-fry and held it for us to see. "They'll be a lot better for you than this stuff. You wait till you taste our home-grown chicken. Besides, chopping off their heads..."

"Could we *please* carry on this debate at some other time, rather than at the dinner table," Dad interrupted, holding up his hand.

He looked at his plate, which didn't seem to appeal to him as much as it had a few minutes ago. I looked at my plate and suddenly realized that all those little chunks of meat had once been part of a live chicken. Like a phantom, a vision of a bloody headless chicken with scaly orange feet pushed its way through the remaining stir-fry and stretched across my plate.

"Excuse me," I said, pushing my chair back

and jumping up. "I have homework to do."

For once, neither Mom nor Dad was critical of me for not finishing my dinner. I ran downstairs and got my books out. Since Grandma had come, she'd taken over my job of clearing the table and doing the dishes. She said she couldn't bear to see them going into a dishwasher that used all that water when she could wash them all in a dishpan full. Who was I to argue? It gave me a bit more time to do homework, and at this time of year, I really appreciated it.

Tonight though, I was finished sooner than I had expected. I had a research project to begin on Monday, but I hadn't chosen a topic yet, so I couldn't work on that. I could study my social studies for the final unit test next week, but I didn't feel like it. For once, I didn't feel like reading a book either. I lay on my bed with my hands behind my head, staring out the window.

I wondered what I would be getting for my birthday tomorrow. I hoped it would be a new mountain bike. I'd certainly dropped a few hints, but I'd had little response to indicate anyone was paying attention. My parents weren't into buying expensive gifts, but maybe just this once...after all, this was a momentous birthday. I was about to turn thirteen. I was about to leave my childhood behind!

I pondered the importance of that for a few moments before deciding it was an occasion for a diary entry. It would have to be a beautifully written entry to mark this turning point in my life. I dug out my dictionary and thesaurus to help. I chewed on my pen for a while, then began to write.

Dear Diary,

A year ago tonight, Wagner and I played with our new Frisbee until we were exhausted. I remember because Dad teased me, saying the new Frisbee was to be my birthday gift. Wagner is gone, and I especially miss him on nights like this, when I remember so vividly precious times we shared.

Tonight is a considerable benchmark in my life, for I turn thirteen at 3:00 a.m. Since I am beginning this new chapter in my book of life, I have chosen to write this entry in a new section of my diary from whence furthermore I shall write.

From this night onward I feel my life shall be changed somehow. I think I'm about to emerge from a stage of metamorphosis. A chrysalis must feel like this when it's about to hatch into a butterfly, or a blossom when it's about to bloom, or even a tadpole who is starting to lose its tail.

Surely when I wake up as a thirteen-year-old, I

will be an altered person. I hope I am smarter, more graceful, more athletic and more beautiful than today. Perhaps it's the suffix "teen" that will make the difference. It sounds ever so much more elegant to say "thirteen" than "twelve". I hope it will cause me to be more sophisticated.

I once read a story about a boy turning thirteen who went through a "rite of passage" where a vision in the form of an animal came to him. The animal brought to him its particular strengths and was his guiding spirit for the rest of his life. I like that idea!

Tonight, Dear Diary, I had a vision on my dinner plate of a headless chicken. I do not want a headless chicken to be my guiding spirit, so I'm going to retire now and concentrate on keeping my mind still until a proper vision comes to me.

In closing, I feel it's an auspicious time to set a goal for my thirteenth year. My goal is to be kissed by a boy. More specifically, I should like to be kissed by Shawn!

Good Night, Dear Diary, this is Nikki signing off at the 11th hour of her 12th year.

I dated my entry before closing it and putting it away in the bottom drawer of my dresser. Then I put on my pjs and climbed into bed. It was early, but if I expected to be visited by my animal vision, I knew I'd better be ready.

Have you ever tried to clear your mind of everything, absolutely everything? It's impossible! I would just about get everything squeezed out, and something else would sneak in behind it. All of a sudden my mind would be full right to the edges with this new thing.

I tried hard to suggest I would like a powerful yet graceful bird such as a hawk or an eagle for my guiding spirit, but neither of them appeared. Instead, I saw rows and rows of new mountain bikes. I suggested to my mind that there were animals I admired for their wisdom and beauty such as a wolf, a coyote or a fox, but I was soon thinking of what it felt like to saw through plywood.

Finally I switched on my lamp and read my book. When I felt my eyes grow heavy, I turned off the light and snuggled down under the blankets. I was swimming between consciousness and sleep, when my vision came to me. A giant crab with knowing black eyes and fierce pincers waving in the air appeared before me. One of his pincers gripped something I couldn't discern.

An ugly old crab couldn't be my guiding force! I tried to chase it out of my mind by concentrating on other things like mountain bikes or sawing plywood, but as hard as I tried to ignore it, or will it away, it wouldn't go. I tried to take away whatever it held in its pincer, but its grip was unbreakable. Finally, exhausted, I gave in and slept.

The crab was the last thing I remember before I awoke as a thirteen-year-old.

9

A snuffling sound nearby woke me. For a moment I lay and listened, too frightened to move. Then there was a small whimpering sound that seemed to originate right outside my door. My clock said 4:00 a.m. Creeping out of bed, I tripped over a pile of books. I hopped over to the door, rubbing my toe as I listened with my ear against the door.

The whimpering stopped. Whatever it was knew that I was on the other side of the door. We both waited. I held my breath for what seemed like an eternity. Then there was an excited whine and a sharp bark.

I yanked the door open and almost gagged at the smell that assaulted me. In front of my feet in a wire cage sat a half-grown black and white dog with a bedraggled red bow at its collar. "Happy Birth..." was all that was left on a chewed up white envelope that had been pulled inside the cage and now lay in the corner, its edge under a large pile of dog poop.

The dog cocked its head at me, whining. It studied me for a second, then eagerly jumped against the cage door, wagging its tail and knocking over its water dish. It danced around, oblivious to the mess under its feet while it continued to bark and whine. Then it sat down and wagged its tail some more.

I held my nose to keep from gagging. "Sh...sh.... Stay still." I climbed over the cage. "Mom...*Mo..om*!" I hollered as loud as I could.

Grandma's door flew open. Groggily, she stuck her head out.

"What the heck?" she muttered. Disappearing for a moment, she reappeared wearing her glasses. Her hair stuck out at all angles, and if I hadn't been so angry, her appearance would have been quite funny.

"I told you I didn't want another dog!" I shouted at her.

Grandma came down the hall, clasping the front of her old worn-out housecoat together. She shook her head.

"I had nothing to do with it," she said sternly. "In fact, I told your mother that it might not be a good idea." She pointed to the cage. "That certainly wasn't a good idea. They didn't tell me they were going to do that!"

"Oh dear, oh dear," my mother's voice murmured behind me. I whirled around to see Mom with Dad behind her. Tousled and sleepy-looking, they both stared at the cage. "Oh, dear!" Mom said again.

I stomped my foot. "Is that all you can say? Look at him. He's a mess! He stinks, and I don't want him. I don't want another dog!"

Grandma bent over the cage and opened the door. "Look at the poor little fellow. It is a boy, isn't it?" She lifted him up high and looked underneath. "Yup, he's a boy all right."

Mom just nodded glumly.

I grabbed my nose again. "Look, it's all over him. He smells horrid. I'm not cleaning him up!" I pushed the cage aside with my foot and backed into my room.

"We thought it would be nice to surprise you," Mom said with a small smile.

"Who needs surprises like that!" I muttered.

Grandma wrinkled her nose and held the pup at arm's length. He sure was a homely thing. His white feet were too big for the rest of him. and his scrawny white-tipped tail was tucked tightly between his legs. He had a white blaze on his face that extended over and around one eye and down his chest, giving him a rather comical appearance. His head and ears were down and his eyes sad. He whimpered pathetically.

"He does smell bad," she said. "All of you go back to bed." She disappeared into the bathroom, still holding the pup in the air, and reappeared with a bottle of shampoo. "This guy's having a bath, then I'm going back to bed too," she said, shuffling down the hall to the laundry room.

Dad took a step towards the cage.

"Put that outside. We'll make do without it. I'll deal with it tomorrow," Grandma said over her shoulder.

I closed my door without saying another word and crawled back into bed. I could hear murmurs of voices, but I didn't care what they were saying. I just felt miserable. I had turned thirteen an hour ago, and since then, pretty much everything had gone downhill!

10

Sunshine streamed through my window, pooling around my head. I stretched like a cat, luxuriating in the fact that I had slept in. It was a few minutes before I remembered the dismal events of early morning.

As I dressed, a pang of guilt nibbled at me. I hadn't behaved very nicely to anyone, and Grandma, through no fault of her own, had ended up taking the brunt of everything. I wondered if she were still sleeping. Then I heard her whistling in the garden. The least I could do was to go out and say "Good morning".

"Happy birthday, thirteen-year-old," she called out when she saw me. "Come and see my lettuce!"

A row of small green plants had pushed their way through the soil overnight.

"Wow! Your garden really is going to grow. Guess you were right," I said.

Grandma bristled. "'Course I'm right. Look, the peas are coming too." She leaned on the hoe and looked at me. "Feeling better?" she asked.

I sighed. "I'm sorry about last night. I didn't mean to be rude. It's just that I don't want another dog. Don't they get it? Wagner can never be replaced!"

"Of course, he can't. But I think you have a big heart. Maybe there's still room in there to love another dog."

I shook my head.

"Well, that's between you and your mom and dad. Maybe he'll have to go back." She scratched her head. "Although, I don't think there's anywhere for him to go."

"What do you mean?"

Grandma shrugged.

"Where is the dog? Where did he sleep?" I asked, more out of curiosity than anything else.

Grandma shrugged again. "Don't know where he is now. He slept in a cardboard box for the rest of the night. He didn't mean any harm. He was just in that darn cage for too long. Thought your parents would know better!"

"They're not used to pups. The last one was Wagner." I looked at the ground. "That was a long time ago."

Grandma hoed at an imaginary weed. "Never mind now. Go and have your breakfast. It won't be long before we have to make the pizza."

"I'll tell Dad to come and look at the garden," I said over my shoulder.

Grandma smiled. "Do that!" she said.

As I was about to go into the house, I saw the pup stretched out in the sun near the rock wall by the garage. I wandered over to have a look at him. The bow was gone, and his coat shone in the sun, giving off the scent of shampoo. He twitched convulsively, chasing something in his puppy dream. Then, sensing someone was near, he opened one eye, lifted his head to sniff and wagged his tail before flopping his head back down. He stretched until he quivered, then rolled over on his back, inviting me to scratch his belly. I was tempted to, but I knew that Grandma could see me from the garden. Besides, if he were going back...

I walked to the house. The pup jumped up and followed me. Bits of gravel clung to his coat, and I bent down to brush them off. As soon as my hand swept along his back, he wiggled against my legs then pounced at me.

"I don't want to play," I said, opening the door. I held up my hand. "Stay!" I said, letting the screen door slam shut behind me. He sat with his head cocked, watching me, until his big feet slid slowly forward, causing him to collapse. He whined, still watching me.

"No," I said, shaking my finger at him. He gave one more short whine as if to have the last word, put his head down on his paws and continued to watch me.

I got a bowl of cereal and sat at the table where I could keep an eye on him. I could hear Mom in the shower. A few minutes later, she appeared, becoming a bit flustered when she saw me. After our early morning encounter, she probably didn't know what to expect.

"Good morning," she said carefully. "Happy birthday."

"Thanks," I said just as carefully. Although I was a little embarrassed by my behaviour in the night, I still felt Mom and Dad had acted insensitively by getting me a dog when they knew how I felt. I just couldn't bring myself to apologize. To my surprise, Mom did.

"I'm sorry you're upset about the dog, Nikki. We shouldn't have done it. It's just that when we went to town for groceries yesterday, I noticed the hubcap place was going out of business, so I stopped to see if he had my hubcap."

"And did he?" I asked, not quite knowing where this was all going.

"Why yes, he did, as a matter of fact. He just hadn't got around to phoning me. As I was leaving, he asked me if I knew of anyone who wanted to buy a pup. He said the runt of the litter was the only one left, and that if someone didn't take it by this Monday, the day he has to vacate the premises, he was going to have it shot."

"Have it shot!" I cried.

"We were horrified as well," Mom said. "He must have too much happening right now with his place going bankrupt and everything. I guess he just couldn't deal with one more problem."

"How could anyone shoot a pup?" I muttered, looking out at him once more. Now I knew what Grandma had meant when she said he had no place to go back to.

Mom reached up on top of the fridge and handed me a present. "This was to be the other part of your gift," she said, sighing.

"I guess we're stuck with him then, right?" I asked as I carefully unwrapped what appeared to be a book. I read the title slowly. *How to Train Your Dog*.

"We could ask around and see if someone else would take him," Mom offered.

Laying the book on the table, I looked at the dog. Then I looked at Mom. "No one else will want him. He's not a cute, cuddly puppy; he's just a homely half-grown runt of a mutt. What kind is he anyway?"

"Your grandmother says he's a Border Collie.

She knows because Border Collies are the dogs they use in Australia to herd sheep."

"Does he have a name?"

Mom smiled. "Well, he does, but you're not going to think much of it. His name is 'Monday'."

"Monday!"

"I know. Pretty silly, if you ask me. I guess the pups were born on a Monday, and when the rest were sold, he didn't know what to call him so he called him 'Monday's Mutt'—'Monday' for short."

"'Mutt' would have been better, but even that's pretty ugly," I said, opening the screen door and looking down at him. "You're one lucky dog! Not only have we saved your life, but we're also going to think of a new name for you." He looked at me quizzically, not sure by the tone of my words if he were being scolded or not. He thumped his tail cautiously.

"Alisha phoned while you were out talking to Grandma," Mom said behind me. "Her Gran is there and has a present for you. Why don't you run down now? Don't be long, though. You have a salad to make. Grandma will want to get started making pizza as well."

"Okay, I'll be back soon." I stepped over the dog and jogged down the driveway. Dad was setting the sprinklers up in the pasture.

"Who's your friend?" he called over, laughing.

I looked over my shoulder. The pup was loping along behind me. I stopped and held up my hand.

"No! Stay!" I ordered. He immediately sat down in the middle of the driveway to look at me. I turned onto the road and looked back. He was still there, head held low, waiting. He looked a little sad.

I sighed. "Oh, all right," I said, beckoning with my hand. "Come on." He sprang forward with a yip and bounced along beside me, looking up every few seconds as if seeking my approval.

"Whose pup?" Alisha cried, looking behind me when she opened the door.

"I guess he's mine," I said tonelessly as she bent to pet him. Alisha quickly looked up at me. I avoided her eyes.

"What's his name?"

I squatted down to pet the pup. He wriggled with joy at having two people lavish attention on him. I thought for a moment.

"'Lucky'...his name is 'Lucky'," I said, decisively.

"He's cute," Alisha offered.

"He's not really cute. He's just a mutt! But he does seem to be quite smart," I replied.

Alisha's Gran appeared at the door. "Happy birthday, dear," she said. Her sweet fragrance wafted over me as she gathered me in her arms for a hug. She stepped back to look at Alisha and myself, standing side by side.

"You two girls are growing like weeds! Why, Nikki, you're taller than I am. How time flies! I hope this little present I got you fits, but of course if it doesn't, we can return it for a larger size."

I gasped as she handed me a beautifully wrapped box. "Thank you, Mrs. Harrison, but you shouldn't have."

"Nonsense! Thirteen is an important birthday to celebrate. Besides, this was just too cute not to buy. I thought it would make you look very feminine."

Carefully removing the bow and wrapping paper, my fingers waded through the neatly folded coloured layers of tissue paper to the beautiful white lacy blouse inside. I held it up in front of me. As I thanked her enthusiastically, I wondered where I would ever wear it. I wasn't sure I wanted to look "more" feminine. The blouse would mostly hang in my closet unused, although I'd have to wear it a few times for Alisha's sake.

When I said I couldn't stay long, Alisha decided to come back with me. I had forgotten about the pup. He was waiting for me, lying on the step, chewing a dog biscuit he'd obviously dug up somewhere in their yard.

For a moment something caught in my throat, and I didn't know whether to laugh or to cry. He stopped chewing on the biscuit and looked at me as if he wasn't sure that what he was doing was okay.

Perhaps allowing Lucky to dig up one of his biscuits was Wagner's way of giving me permission to love another dog, I thought. Maybe this was his way of saying goodbye.

I lifted Lucky into my arms and hugged him tightly. "You are just too smart for your own good," I whispered into his ear. He didn't lick me, as a lot of dogs would have done. He just jammed his snout into my ear and snuffled and wiggled until I set him back down.

11

W hat did you get for your birthday?" Alisha asked as we trod up the hill to our place.

I looked straight ahead on the road. "Well, I got Lucky, and a book on how to train him." I looked down at him trotting along side of us, tongue hanging out. "Although I'm not sure I'll need it. He seems to be training himself."

"What did you get from your Grandma?" Alisha asked.

"Nothing," I replied without hesitation. "She would never buy something just for a birthday. She doesn't believe in buying things unless you absolutely need them."

"Yeah, I can see she'd be like that," Alisha said thoughtfully. "She's different from anyone I know, but I like her."

I nodded my head slowly.

Shawn arrived just as we started making pizza, so Grandma had the opportunity to show all three of us how to make pizza. Each of us wanted different toppings, so it ended up loaded with all sorts of goodies. We heaped onions, garlic, shrimp, red pepper, fresh tomatoes, mushrooms, pepperoni and of course, lots of cheese on it. I asked if we could make a dessert pizza like one I'd tasted once in a restaurant, but Grandma wasn't sure what went on it, so we dug through the cupboards and found what we thought would work. We baked a crust first, then spread chocolate hazelnut sundae topping over it and heaped lots of fresh fruit on top.

"Mmm, smells good," Dad said, passing through the kitchen as the buzzer on the oven went. "I'm getting hungry."

I carefully lifted out the cookie sheet that held the pizza. It looked delicious. We had grated extra cheese on top, which had toasted to a bubbly golden perfection.

"I'll take it out to the patio," I said. "Grab the juice and glasses, will you please, Shawn, and Alisha, can you get the plates and serviettes?"

Grandma held the door open with the bowl of salad and dressing I'd made earlier. By the time Shawn, Alisha and Grandma had set their things on the patio table, there wasn't room for the cookie sheet. I set it on the bench beside the table. Grandma said I should have the honour of cutting it, since not only was it my birthday, but it was the first whole meal I'd ever prepared.

My knife sank into the bubbling cheese. Steam and hot tomato sauce oozed out and onto my fingers. "Ouch!" I hollered, dropping the knife. "We'll have to leave it a few minutes to cool."

"While we're waiting, let's go in and open your presents," Alisha said, clapping her hands. We all trooped back inside to the living room, where Mom and Dad were sitting, trying, no doubt, to stay out of our way until they were called for pizza.

Most kids like to unwrap presents as fast as they can, one right after the other, but I like to savour mine one at a time. It's probably because I usually get so few that it would all be over too quickly unless I did take the time to "ooh" and "ahh" over each one.

The first one to be unwrapped was from Shawn. It was three of the *Redwall* series of books. Fantasy is one of my favourite genres, so everyone listened while I read the first page of each book.

The next two presents were from Alisha. The first was a CD she knew I'd wanted, and inside a little box, wrapped in gold foil with a beautiful bow on top, was a pair of gold stud earrings.

"They're beautiful! I don't have pierced ears though, you know," I said, holding back my long hair to show her my ear.

"I know," Alisha said, laughing, "but I thought it would be fun if we both got them done together. If you don't want to, though," she said hastily, seeing the uncertainty on my face, "I can take them back and get you something else."

I had never thought about the possibility of somebody punching a hole through my ear. I asked her to give me a few days to think about it.

I unwrapped a pair of jeans and a T-shirt from Mom and Dad. I had a feeling this was an "extra" they had gone to buy this afternoon to make up for my earlier disappointment. I hugged them both.

"There's one you almost missed," Alisha said, pointing under the loose wrapping paper that had come off the other gifts.

I picked up a little box wrapped in newspaper. It had no writing on the outside to indicate whom it was from. I held it for a moment. There was only one person who would wrap a gift in newspaper. I looked at Grandma.

She smiled one of her rare smiles. "Open it, girl. Don't stand looking at it."

I opened it slowly, my mind in a whirl. I knew she wouldn't have bought anything. What could it possibly be? I lifted the lid of a well-worn box to see a delicate gold chain inside. I carefully held it up for everyone to see and looked at

Grandma questioningly.

"My mother gave that to me when I turned thirteen. I don't wear jewellery any more, so thought it would be fitting for you to have on your thirteenth birthday."

"Oh, Iris," my mom said. "That's very old and probably very valuable. Are you sure?"

"'Course I'm sure, or I wouldn't have done it. It will just be one less thing to worry about." She took it from me and placed it around my neck. "Nikki will look after it."

I turned around to admire it in the mirror.

"Wow," Alisha whispered, looking at me in the mirror. I could tell she was green with envy.

"Cool," Shawn said, looking up from reading one of the books he had given me.

"Thank you, Grandma," I said, letting the chain glide through my fingers. It felt like it belonged there. I would take care of it!

"If we wait any longer, we'll have to reheat that pizza," Grandma said. "I'll bring out the dessert one as well."

We stepped onto the patio just in time to see Lucky standing up on his hind legs at the bench, his mouth full of pizza as he tried to drag it off the cookie sheet. Before I could shout, the whole pizza slid off the cookie sheet, broke in half, and landed face down on the ground. Onions, garlic, shrimp, red pepper, fresh tomatoes, mushrooms, pepperoni and tomato sauce flew in every direction. Lucky tried to leap out of the way, but not before he was covered in tomato sauce. He grabbed one of the broken pieces and was about to drag it away when I found my voice.

"Drop it. Bad dog!" I hollered.

He dropped it immediately and looked at us guiltily. Then, instead of running away and hiding, as any sensible dog would have done, he hung his head. Whining and crawling on his belly, he grovelled his way towards us.

"Oh, our pizza!" I moaned, stepping over him and surveying the mess. I looked back at Lucky. "Bad dog! Should I spank him?"

Alisha began to giggle. "Look at him! How could you spank that?"

"Don't spank him," Shawn said, laughing too. "It was our own fault for leaving the pizza out here. He probably thought we'd set up a banquet table just for him."

"I think it's a good thing I bought you that book," Mom said, disappearing into the house for the broom and a pail. "You're going to need it."

"Humph!" Grandma snorted. "I think he's already read one himself on how to train people. Look at him trying to plead 'not guilty' while covered in evidence!"

"Now we'll never know how good Nikki's first pizza was," Dad muttered, "and I don't know about any of you, but I'm hungry. I'll go phone in an order and have it delivered."

"We've still got our dessert pizza. We'll just eat our meal backwards," I said, watching Shawn wipe the tomato sauce off Lucky with a serviette.

"At least, you've had a birthday to remember!" Mom said, frowning as she shovelled our wonderful pizza into the garbage.

It really was a birthday to remember, I thought to myself much later when I was in bed trying to go to sleep. First, there had been the surprise arrival of Lucky, then the pizza fiasco, and the unexpected gift from Grandma. To top it off, Mom and Dad had come to my room to say "good night" a while ago.

"I know you wanted a new mountain bike, Nikki," Mom said, "but we just couldn't afford it right now."

"That's okay. It was a good birthday with lots of unexpected surprises," I said, sitting up and hugging my knees.

Dad chuckled. "You can say that again!" He rubbed his chin. "About the bike...we have another idea for you to consider."

"Really? What's that?"

"Well, our neighbour from across the way

wants to rent our extra pasture for his cows. The fence isn't in very good shape, so he wants them home at night. They'd also need water. I told him you might be interested in the job of bringing the cows over each day and returning them in the evening, as well as keeping them watered. You could save the money you earn towards a new mountain bike."

"Wow," I said, "my first job. Sure, Ginger and I can do it."

"What about this guy? He'd probably like to help," Dad said, looking down at Lucky, who tonight was staying in my room. He was fast asleep in his cardboard box, no doubt tuckered out from all the mischief he'd caused since his arrival.

"Yeah, right! I'm not letting him anywhere near those cows!" I wasn't sure what disaster Lucky would become involved in concerning the cows, but I was determined to keep this job so I could buy that mountain bike.

12

The next day I rode back to the pond with Shawn to look for more pins. When we were saddled up and ready to start off, Lucky appeared. He looked up at me and whined. At least this time he was asking permission to do something.

I debated whether to carry him in the saddle with me or to let him run along behind us. We decided it would be better for him to be on the ground, so that he could become familiar with the area. I was a little worried, because he was not used to the horses. He might get underfoot and either get kicked or stepped on, but he quickly proved himself to be alert and aware of where he was in relationship to the horses. Every minute or so he'd run up beside Ginger to make eye contact with me before disappearing again into the ditch. The white tip of his black tail weaving through the grass was the only indication of the path his nose was taking him on.

It was evident there had been more people around the pond area since our last visit. Several branches had been broken by someone walking through, and footprints had been left along the pond's muddy shore. We explored the immediate area for some time but did not come across any more red tape or surveyor's pins.

"I wonder what's up," Shawn said as we sat for a few minutes before riding home again.

I yawned, leaning back against the tree. "More people than just us have to know about this area. They're probably just coming here to enjoy the turtles, like we do," I said, stroking Lucky, who had finally played himself out and was napping beside us.

"Maybe," said Shawn doubtfully.

"Look!" I said, sitting forward and pointing at the pond. A mother duck swam in front of eight fluffy yellow ducklings. They talked in quiet quacking voices as they swam around the turtles' log towards the bulrushes on the other side. Lucky, awake now, lowered his head and lay like a statue, watching them.

When they reached shore, the mother duck waddled out, wiggled her tail and quacked for her babies to follow. As each one left the water, it too wiggled its tail. They disappeared into the bushes.

It was time for us to go home. We untied the horses and were getting ready to mount when I realized Lucky wasn't in view. As I was about to call him, the mother duck with her babies appeared. They were running as a group— first one direction, then another. I soon saw the reason. Lucky was behind them, crouched low. Something told me he wasn't about to pounce on them, but the mother duck was becoming frantic, and I didn't wait to find out. I called him back. She quickly turned about and led the ducklings to the safety of the water.

"What was he up to this time?" Shawn asked, leading the way out.

"I'm not sure," I said, watching Lucky run to me. "He's a bit of a pain, though. It seems like you have to watch him every second."

Shawn chuckled. "It's kind of like babysitting, isn't it?"

Mom and Dad were making dinner when I got home. My parents and my grandmother had come to a silent agreement over mealtimes soon after her arrival. They did the meal preparation, while she stayed out of the way, then she did the clean up and the dishes while they cleared out. I think it was because none of them could agree on the way either job should be done.

As I went to my room, I noticed Grandma

sitting in the rocking chair in the TV room with a large book open on her lap. She was so involved in looking at it, she didn't hear me approach.

"What are you looking at?" I asked, causing her to jump.

She closed the book and hugged it to her chest. "Oh, it's just a scrapbook I've kept over the years," she said lightly.

"Can I look at it?" I was keen on knowing what my grandmother would find interesting enough to keep a scrapbook on.

She hesitated, as though a bit embarrassed. "I guess so," she said, continuing to hug the book.

"If you don't want to show me, that's okay."

"No...it's all right," she said, offering the book to me. "It's just that no one else has ever seen it."

"Why not?"

"I guess I never had anyone else to show it to."

I sat down on the floor cross-legged with the book, aware that Grandma was watching me as she leaned back in her chair.

It became evident very quickly that this was a record of her life in Australia. The first couple of pages were pictures of her soon after she had arrived, judging from the dates written underneath.

"Was this your husband?" I asked, pointing to the weathered, middle-aged man at her side in one of the photos.

Leaning forward to look at the picture, she smiled. "Yes, that was us just after we got married. Jim had been working to protect the area around where he lived for the declining population of koalas."

"Really?" I asked. "Why was it declining?"

"We lived in a very popular area of southern Australia. As development took place, no one seemed to care about the koalas, who had always made their home there. As well as once being hunted almost to extinction for their fur," she went on, "koalas had been threatened by disease and bushfires, so it was really important for us to do this."

I flipped the pages, reading a couple of newspaper articles, one of which included a snap of Grandma holding a koala.

"They're so cute! No wonder you wanted to protect them," I said, holding the book up to have a closer look.

"We were successful, thanks mainly to Jim, who had worked so hard before I met him. They're now able to carry on in their own little spot of wilderness," she said, smiling.

I turned to the next page.

"That was our biggest project," Grandma said, her eyes lighting up. She sat down on the floor beside me. "We spent the last eight years trying to protect the cassowary." Grandma pointed to the clipping, which contained a picture of an extremely large bird with a funny looking growth on the top of its head.

"Wow! They look huge. What's that on its head?"

"They're actually the largest land animal in Australia, despite being a bird. They stand two metres tall and weigh up to eighty kilograms. That growth on their head is like a horn helmet. It protects their head as they run through the thick rainforests where they live." She ran her fingers over the picture affectionately. "There are fewer than fifteen hundred of them left in the world. Their survival is crucial because they spread many of the rainforest seeds."

"What did you do to try and save them?" I asked, eager to hear more about this unusual bird.

"We fought hard over the years to make the bureaucrats and the public realize what we were doing was important. Then we organized and taught a group of seniors who were interested in running the Environmental Centre we built."

"You built an Environmental Centre?" I asked in disbelief.

Grandma nodded. "With lots of help, we did. I felt it was a good way to spend my money. Now tourists as well as local people will realize how important the survival of the cassowary really is."

"Wow, what an accomplishment!" I said.

Grandma leaned back against the rocking chair. "We never looked at it that way. It just needed to be done, so we did it," she said.

"Why haven't you ever talked about all this?" I asked, waving my hands to indicate the scrapbook and what it contained. "I had no idea. I'm sure Mom and Dad..."

"Your mom and dad don't often understand my way of looking at things," Grandma interrupted. "Besides, there's no use talking about something. It's actions that count."

I came to the last page of newspaper clippings and photos. It was a page full of information on her husband's life. It also contained his obituary. After reading it, I closed the book softly. "It must have been hard to leave Australia after all the two of you had done," I said.

Grandma took the book I offered her and got up stiffly. She looked away, her eyes misty. "I guess the challenge of it all died with him," she said quietly, "and I was kind of worn out. When he passed away, I felt the need to be around family again."

I followed Grandma upstairs. After dinner, I went for a walk with Lucky to try and sort out things in my head. I thought a lot about Grandma's scrapbook and what she'd done in Australia. The thing that kept running through my mind, though, was her statement about her need to be around family. Before this, I'd never thought of my grandmother as a needy person.

13

Summer holidays were approaching with a little over a week of school left. We were all getting a bit rambunctious at school. It's hard to maintain your cool as well as your concentration when you're so close to the end. I was doing my best though, because it was evident Dad was beginning to feel frazzled, and I didn't want to change the relationship we'd been able to maintain ever since the incident concerning the math test.

To keep the class focussed, Dad had assigned a research project for the last week of school. I decided to do mine on the kind of turtle that lived in Watson's Pond, so I could learn more about them.

I'd gone on the Internet the night before and found that they are called the Western Painted Turtle. I'd also brought a bunch of books home from the school library to make notes from.

On our way home from school, we'd checked

the robin's nest. Five little bald heads with gaping mouths greeted us as we parted the branches. They must have hatched overnight. Knowing that the parents were nearby collecting food for them, we left quickly.

I was anxious to see the chicks that had arrived today. Grandma was right. They were half-grown, and their fluffy down was almost gone. Red combs were appearing on their heads, and their wings were already sprouting pinfeathers. We were keeping them enclosed for the first couple of days. Then Grandma wanted to allow them free range of the yard.

"Makes for better tasting chicken, and for better eggs," she told me.

"Ugh," I thought.

"Why does everything that arrives here have to be half-grown?" I muttered, watching them run around the pen.

"I was a little more than half-grown when I arrived," Grandma said.

I laughed. "I mean the chickens and Lucky," I said, bending to pet him. He seemed fascinated by the chickens. He lay close to the fence, his head low, watching them as they moved about the pen.

"Well, what about those baby robins down the road?" Grandma asked as she put feed in the trays and filled the plastic waterer.

"They're young, but they're ugly—nothing but a bald head with a big mouth!" I said.

"I know. I saw them myself today. But they'll become cuter as they grow."

"Do you think Lucky will want to hurt the chickens?" I asked.

Grandma thought for a moment. "I think he's smart enough to know they're ours and not to be touched. We'll have to watch him to make sure, though."

"I'm going to leave Lucky here with you while I go round up the cows to take them home," I said, holding up my hand as a signal for him to stay.

My first day on the job hadn't been as easy as I'd thought it would be. I'd had to get up a half-hour earlier than usual in order to move the cows to our pasture before doing my other chores and getting ready for school. Rather than saddle up Ginger, I'd decided to ride her bareback. Big mistake! As all of this was new to the cows, they all wanted to run in different directions instead of going out the neighbour's gate and along the road to our pasture. As Ginger wheeled back and forth a couple of times chasing one who had run in the wrong direction, I lost my balance and nearly slid off.

And I'd met "Ms. Fancypants"! I gave her that

name because her brown markings stretched up over her back legs and rear-end to stop midway across her back and belly. It looked just like a pair of brown pants she'd pulled on. I was so busy looking at the "pants" that I didn't notice she also carried a large set of pointed horns. She wasn't about to move. Every time Ginger got near her, she'd snort, lower her head and stare menacingly in our direction.

I decided to ignore her and rode around her, getting the rest out of the gate. When she realized she was going to be left behind, she let out a long mournful "moo". With a switch of her tail, she ambled out the gate behind the others.

By the time I got back to the house, it was later than I'd planned. I'd barely made it to school on time. For the rest of the week I was going to have to get up even earlier!

That evening I was glad I had time to saddle Ginger as the task turned out to be even more difficult than in the morning. The cows did not want to leave the pasture to go home. By the time I'd get a few of them started in the right direction, the others would run off in opposite directions. I ended up making two trips, taking the willing ones first and closing the gate behind me. Then I came back to get the rest. Once again I had to deal with "Ms. Fancypants". She hadn't wanted to come to the pasture in the first place. Now she didn't want to go back. By the time I got home I was tired and cranky.

"Stupid cows!" I muttered, flopping onto the couch next to Dad, who was reading the newspaper. "I'm sure they must have a brain the size of a pea."

Dad laughed. "I never said the job would be easy. Don't forget you're being paid pretty well."

The vision of the mountain bike floated in my head. "Yeah, I know. I'll survive."

Dad read silently for a few minutes. Then he looked over the newspaper at me. "Imagine that! A ritzy housing development is going in fairly near to us."

"Oh, yeah? Where?" I said yawning. All I wanted to do was go to bed. It seemed like I'd spent my whole day chasing cows.

"Apparently over by Watson's pond."

"What!" I sat bolt upright. "That can't be! It's just a bunch of wilderness and a swampy pond."

"Not for long," Dad said. "It's an eighty-acre parcel of land. It's going to be made into exclusive one-acre lots."

"But there's a family of turtles living in the pond, and today we saw a family of ducks," I cried. "They're not going to be very happy having all those houses around. Does that mean we won't be able to ride in that area any more?"

Dad shrugged, looking at me sympathetically. "Unfortunately, you can't stop what other people consider to be progress, Nikki." Then he smiled. "In this case, if the developer knows what he's doing, in all probability it will be an asset to the neighbourhood. It could bring up our property value a lot."

"How can it be an asset to our neighbourhood if it gobbles up land that wild animals are living on? They were here first, just like Grandma's koalas!" I said angrily, getting up. Dad looked up at me, surprised, but I didn't offer any further explanation. There was no use, just as there was no use arguing with him over this. He was tired, I was tired, and we saw things differently.

Before going to bed, I showered. I didn't do any of the research I'd planned on doing. I unburdened all my angry feelings about the unfairness of it all on Lucky, who had somehow ended up sleeping on my bed over the last few days. He appeared to listen, his head cocked, one paw resting over my arm. Then, with a whine of sympathy, he put his head down and slept. I lay awake for a very long time.

14

I was too busy over the next week to give a lot of thought to the pond or to ride over to it. I hardly even saw Alisha or Shawn outside of school. I was working hard to complete my research on time. We'd all chosen very different topics to research. Shawn had decided on China, as he hoped to go there some day, and Alisha was interested in researching some of the top fashion designers, so there was no way I could work together with either of them.

My job seemed to take the rest of my time. Ms. Fancypants continued to be ornery, adding extra time and the need for patience each time I moved the cows. I was very much looking forward to school being out so I'd finally have more time to myself.

Grandma had decided to let the chickens have their free range a few days after their arrival. I reminded her to watch Lucky, but I needn't have bothered. He spent most of his day with her while I was at school. He would sleep in the garden as she worked, and later she would take him for a walk to see the baby robin's progress.

I had told her about Watson's pond and the proposed development. Today she and Lucky had walked over to it. When I got home from school she told me that nothing more had been done. She had other news for me as well.

"The chickens finally wandered over and found the garden today," she told me, laughing. "Lucky wouldn't let them near. In fact, he kept taking them back to the chicken house. I guess he thinks that's where they belong."

I looked at Lucky who was lying on my bed beside me as I worked my way through the turtle books.

"You mean he chased them?" I asked, surprised.

"Not really. It was more like friendly persuasion. I think Lucky has the Border Collie herding instinct. He never barked or nipped at them. He just crawled along on his belly behind them as long as they were going in the direction he wanted them to go. As soon as one headed off in another direction, he'd circle around it and herd it back. He's pretty young. He could become very good at it."

"I guess that's what he was trying to do with a mother duck and her babies over at the pond," I told her. "I called him off just in case."

She laughed. "The mother duck would have probably taken him on if he'd been up to no good." She sat on the edge of the bed and stroked Lucky, who thumped his tail appreciatively.

"What are you doing?" she asked, picking up one of the books on turtles.

"I'm working on a research project for school. I decided to research the Western Painted Turtle, because they live over at the pond."

"They used to live all over this area. They were often seen crawling along the road where I lived, but I guess there aren't many left," Grandma said, sighing.

"I guess not. The only place I've seen them is over at the pond. I sure hope they'll be okay when that subdivision goes in," I said.

Grandma stood up. "Don't count on it. If those turtles mean a lot to you, you'd better keep an eye on what's going on over there."

"I will," I said, "but there's not much I can do about it if I don't like what's happening."

Grandma just raised an eyebrow but didn't say anything. When she turned to leave, she ran her hand over a large tear in the seat of her worn jeans.

"By the way, is there a Thrift Store in town?" she asked.

"A Thrift Store? I think so. Why?"

"'Cause I ripped the rear-end out of my jeans today. I've had these for a few years. Guess I need another pair," she said.

It was the only pair of pants I'd seen her in since her arrival. Surely she didn't plan on replacing them with a pair of used ones.

I thought for a moment. "I...I have some money saved. Why don't I just give you enough for a pair of new jeans?"

Grandma snorted. "Don't be silly, girl. I don't need your money. That's not the point. Why buy a new pair when there are plenty of good used ones around?" She looked at her faded, well-worn shirt. "Might just about be time for a couple of shirts as well."

I was silent. It wasn't my idea of shopping, but when I thought about it, I just couldn't see my grandmother in new clothes bought at a shopping mall.

I finished taking notes out of the books I'd got from the library before going upstairs to make some hot chocolate. Mom was sitting at the kitchen table, busy marking papers.

"Should I get my ears pierced, Mom?" I asked.

I'd been thinking about it ever since I'd received the pair of gold studs from Alisha. Every night I'd have another look at them and try to imagine what it felt like to have a hole punched through your ear. I was pretty sure I had decided what I was going to do, but it's always wise to ask about these things. Parents like to think they have a say in your decisions.

Yawning, Mom put her red pen down and stretched her arms over her head. This was always a tiring time of the year for her.

"Well, if you really think you need another couple of holes in your head, I guess it's all right." I winced. She smiled. "I'm just teasing. They're nice earrings, and they'd look good with the necklace Grandma gave you."

I let the chain slide through my fingers. "Yeah, I know. I'll give it some more thought," I said, giving her a goodnight kiss.

15

Finally, the last day of school arrived. It was an extra early one for me. Our school was hosting a pancake breakfast in the parking lot for students, parents and staff. The grade sevens were responsible for setting up the tables and were to be there by seven-thirty. I had set my alarm for a half-hour earlier than my already early rising time. When it buzzed at five-thirty, I sat up dazed for a moment, not knowing where I was. The rising sun filled the room with a rosy glow. Beside me, Lucky whined softly without lifting his head. It was just too early! I rolled over and went back to sleep.

The next thing I knew, Lucky was standing over me shoving his nose in my face, his tail fanning the air in a good morning wag. I sat up groggily to look at the alarm clock. Omigosh! I'd slept the whole extra half-hour I'd set for myself to be away to school on time. I leapt out of bed, practically throwing on my clothes as I ran quietly for the door so I wouldn't wake Grandma.

Once again, I didn't have time to saddle Ginger. I slipped on her bridle and jumped on her bare back. With a slight touch of my heels, we were off. The air was already thick with heat. It had been building all week, getting hotter each day. While the sun was up in the east, the west was full of threatening purple banks of clouds.

The cows seemed to sense the possible change in the weather and didn't want to leave the security of home. They began milling around in confusion—no one willing to take the lead out of the gate.

At my urging, Ginger darted back and forth to try and point them in the right direction, but they became more uncertain and alarmed. Over the past couple of weeks, she had learned what her job was, and now she sometimes moved on her own, which made it even harder to keep my balance.

Ms. Fancypants took up her usual stance, facing us, her back to the rest. The confusion behind her appeared to agitate her more than usual. In the past few weeks, Ginger had also learned that Ms. Fancypants was a bluffer. She would only stand her ground for so long if we continued to walk towards her. Then she would turn and trot out behind the others.

Today the weather must have been getting to Ginger as well, or maybe the cows were. For whatever reason, she wasn't in the mood to play the usual game and broke into a trot toward Ms. Fancypants. For once, the cow did not turn and run. Rather, she lowered her horns, switched her tail and took a menacing step towards us.

Alarmed, Ginger suddenly jumped sideways. Without any warning, I slid off her back and landed with a dull thud a few metres in front of Ms. Fancypants. She stood glaring at me and lowered her horns even more. I froze in fear.

Suddenly the group of cows behind her split in the middle and ran in opposite directions. Lucky burst through the cloud of dust, running towards me, his tongue hanging out, his tail beating wildly in the air. Somehow, he'd escaped from the house, where I usually left him while I did the cows. He probably had no idea of what was happening at that moment. He was just happy to see me. He raced around Ms. Fancypants, then sensing her threat to me, he turned to face her.

Without hesitating, he ran at her, barking sharply. She lowered her horns to the ground and charged at us, trying to gore Lucky, but he dodged her horns and snaked around behind her as if to nip her heels. Snorting, she whirled about and ran towards the gate.

"Good dog, Lucky!" I shouted, getting up rather shakily and brushing the dust off me. "Good dog!"

With that encouragement, he seemed to know Ms. Fancypants was supposed to continue out the gate. He made sure she did by forcing her to change direction whenever she veered towards the other cows. Once he had her out the gate, he ran back to me as if checking to see what he was to do next.

Ginger was standing nearby, the reins lying in the dirt. I gathered them up and, jumping back on her, we went after the other cows. That was all Lucky needed to know. He darted towards them, yipping at them to tell them he meant business. When one of them looked like she was thinking of not following the rest, he streaked around the back and urged her on. He ran from side to side, yipping with excitement, until he had them all out the gate as a group, while Ginger and I watched in amazement.

"Okay, Lucky. Easy now. We don't want a stampede on our hands," I called, hurrying to catch up. But the cattle weren't all that frightened. They seemed to sense they were being directed rather than being chased. As long as they went where they were supposed to go, there was no problem with this little black and white ball of energy that had suddenly come into their lives.

"Why didn't I let you try that earlier?" I said to Lucky, hugging him after we had the cows safely in the pasture and Ginger in her own. "I could have been having twenty minutes more sleep every morning!" Lucky just sat there, his tongue hanging out panting, but as he looked up at me his eyes seemed to shine with happiness.

Grandma was right. He did have a natural herding instinct, and he loved the job! Well, from now on, he could do it. Grandma had told me there were verbal commands as well as whistle signals to teach herding dogs. Maybe she knew what they were and would help me teach them to Lucky. It was important for him to learn that while he was directing the animals, I was directing him.

*   *   *

When our report cards were handed out later that morning, just before year-end dismissal, I held mine for a few moments, afraid to open it. I'd completed my research two days ago and felt that I'd done a thorough and good job of it. I'd even contacted local wildlife people for more information. Although we hadn't found out our mark for that paper yet, it would be reflected on the report card as part of our Language Arts mark. I knew that math wouldn't be a problem. I mentally ran through the rest of my subjects but still hesitated to open the envelope.

"Look at this Nikki. I got all As except for a C in French," Shawn said, looking crestfallen for a moment. Then he brightened. "Oh well, it's China I'm interested in. At least I got an A in Language Arts from that report I did."

Alisha was usually happy with her report card. She excelled in Math, was a hard worker and always seemed to maintain a good, if not top average. She smiled as she looked at her marks. I glanced at them. All Bs and an A in Math.

"Come on, Nikki. Open yours," she urged. I could tell that Dad was watching me out of the corner of his eye. I slowly pulled the report card from the envelope and opened it. I couldn't believe my eyes. I had achieved straight As! I breathed a great sigh of relief.

"Congratulations!" Shawn whooped, giving me a high five.

"Way to go," Alisha shouted, grabbing me in a hug. Some of the other kids crowded around to congratulate me as well. I was happy that they didn't seem to feel I'd been given those marks because my dad was also my teacher. Most of them knew how hard I'd worked to bring up my marks this past term. I glanced up at Dad, who was smiling. I knew he would congratulate me later in private.

"Guess what?" I said to Alisha as she and Shawn and I trudged up the hill in the muggy heat. "I've decided to get my ears pierced."

"Really?" Alisha squealed. "That's great! Let's make an appointment for tomorrow if we can. I'll make it."

"Okay," I said slowly. I was still feeling a little uncertain about it, so it was a good thing Alisha was going to make the appointment. I just might never get around to it.

We stopped in the shade of the trees along the road for a rest and to check on the robins. Their bald heads and previously naked ugly bodies had fuzzed over with down. When they saw us, they all stretched their necks out and opened their mouths wide, making us laugh. As they gradually realized we weren't there to deliver food, they closed their mouths and slumped back into a mass of little heads that filled the nest. It wouldn't be long until they would outgrow it.

We left Alisha at her driveway. I was anxious to go over to the pond as I hadn't been there for a few days, but Alisha said it was too hot, and she'd call me later after she'd made our appointment.

Shawn was as upset as I was over the proposed development. He decided to take his books home and said he'd meet me in an hour. Because of the heat, we would walk over. Besides, my backside was still smarting from falling off Ginger that morning. I'd had enough riding for one day. I ran to find Grandma and tell her all the exciting news.

16

"D o you think they're really going ahead with it? Nothing more has happened since our last visit to the pond," I said as we drove into town the next day.

Grandma and Dad were both out to buy a pair of pants, Grandma of course from the Thrift Shop, and Dad from his favourite men's clothing store. He said jokingly that he was going to treat himself after a hard year of teaching his own daughter. Alisha and I had our appointment to get our ears pierced. Mom had stayed home to sleep, thankful I'm sure that for once she had nothing that needed doing.

"What would stop them?" Grandma snipped from the back seat. She looked at the back of Dad's head as if she were speaking to him. "You can be sure it's not for the benefit of the neighbourhood either. There's a lot of money to be made there."

Dad ignored her. "I'm sure it's going ahead,

Nikki. These things just take time. Enjoy your riding while you can, because I don't know if you'll have access to the pond once the development is finished."

"Just as long as they don't hurt those turtles," I muttered. Since learning so much about them for my report, I felt I really knew them. They seemed almost like a part of my family.

"Like I said before," Grandma warned, "if those turtles mean a lot to you, you'd better keep an eye on what's going on over there."

Dad shook his head and began whistling tunelessly.

First, we stopped at the Thrift Shop for Grandma. Dad said he'd stay in the car to listen to CDs, but Alisha and I decided it might be fun to go with Grandma. We just hoped we wouldn't meet anyone we knew.

She quickly picked out another pair of jeans and two shirts. One shirt looked almost new. I couldn't believe the amount of clothing in the store. I had to admit most of it looked not bad, but it all seemed to have a stale smell.

"You'd smell stale too if you had to hang around with all these other clothes waiting to be chosen. A little detergent and sunshine will fix that," Grandma said as she counted out six dollars in change and took the clothing in a recycled paper bag.

"Six dollars. That's pretty good," I said, climbing into the car.

"Yup," Grandma agreed, "but cost isn't the issue. Every time I walk into a shopping mall, I can't for the life of me figure out where all that stuff eventually ends up. Most likely in a landfill." She sniffed. "It's just my way of not adding to the problem."

I looked at Alisha, but I think it all went over her head. She loved shopping. Dad was whistling again, so I knew he was shutting out Grandma's logic. I wasn't quite ready to buy my clothes from a Thrift Shop, but I was sure that from now on, whenever I walked into a shopping mall, I would be reminded of Grandma's words.

Our next stop was at Dad's store. Grandma said she would walk to the library and meet us later, but Dad insisted he'd like three ladies' opinions rather than two, so she patiently sat and waited while he tried on a few pairs of pants, deciding on one pair with help from all of us. They were far too long and needed hemming.

"Seven dollars just to hem a pair of pants. That's ridiculous. Won't take me twenty minutes," Grandma muttered. Dad quickly paid for the pants minus hemming, much to the amusement of the shopkeeper, I think.

We finally got to our appointment just before lunch. I'd been sort of dreading it, but not Alisha. She marched ahead of me into the shop and offered to go first. She was dying to look glamorous! It turned out to be not as bad as I'd expected. A sharp pain and it was over, except for instructions on how to avoid infection and the warning that I would likely feel some discomfort for a few days. Because the earrings that Alisha had given me were made of gold, they were inserted right away. I tied my long hair into a loose knot behind my ears before we came out of the shop. I suddenly felt a bit more grown up.

"Wow, look at these two ladies, would you?" Dad teased.

"To each her own," Grandma said, which I think meant that she would never do anything so foolish, but if I wanted to—well, that was up to me. She smiled. "They do look nice with the necklace. Do your ears hurt?"

"A little," I said. The truth was, they'd started throbbing. Right after lunch and as soon as we got home, I planned on applying ice to each one.

Mom said they looked great. She suggested I might want to think about getting my hair cut short again to show them off. She even offered to pay for it—a delayed birthday gift, she said. I was quick to accept. I'd been planning on getting it cut for the summer anyway, and would have paid for it myself. Now my money could continue to build towards my bike.

On the way home, I'd also been thinking of another way to save money.

"Mom, can you teach me to sew this summer?"

She looked up from the book she was reading. "What do you want to sew?" she asked.

"Well, I know I'll need new clothes for school this fall. If I could make something, I'd save a lot of money, right? Besides, it would be different from what anyone else has."

Mom nodded. "Some things are complicated to sew. I haven't made anything for years."

"I know, but couldn't we start off with something easy?" I asked.

Grandma was sitting at the table thumbing through a magazine. "Tell you what," she interjected. "I was just going to shorten your dad's pants. Learning how to do that would be a good start."

I looked at Mom.

"Sounds good to me," she said. Perhaps the thought of teaching me to sew during her summer off wasn't that appealing.

Grandma sent me to set up the ironing board while she found a tape measure, scissors and pins.

The tailor had loosely pinned the pant legs to the right length when Dad had tried them on. Grandma measured the length pinned up. "Sixteen centimetres," she said. "We need to leave about four centimetres to turn up for the hem, so we'll cut off twelve centimetres."

She pulled out the tailor's pins and smoothed one leg flat against the ironing board. While she watched, she told me what to do. I was to measure from the bottom of the leg twelve centimetres up and place a pin. By doing this all around the leg, I would have a guide to follow when I cut.

I nervously measured and pinned my way around the leg, paying close attention to what she'd said so as not to make a mistake on Dad's new pants.

"That looks good," she said, inspecting my work closely. "Now just cut carefully from pin to pin around the leg, then do the same on the other one." She settled onto a stool nearby.

I took the scissors and very carefully began cutting. I was starting to enjoy this and decided that making some clothes for myself should be easy.

"Did you ever have a Border Collie, Grandma?" I asked, continuing to cut.

"Yup. Had one in Australia. Lucky reminds me a lot of him, as a matter of fact, although he didn't have the white ring around his eye that Lucky has. He was a beautiful dog!" She leaned over to inspect my cutting. "Now pay attention and watch what you're doing."

"I am, don't worry." I cut to the last pin and removed the piece of the leg I'd cut off. "See how straight my cutting is," I said, holding the piece up for her to see. As I took my hands off the pants, they slid off the ironing board and landed in a heap on the floor. I quickly picked them up.

"Yup. Looks good. Now, do the other leg exactly the same." She said, leaning back again.

"What was his name?" I asked as I smoothed the leg onto the board and started measuring and pinning again.

"Who?" Grandma asked.

"Your Border Collie."

"Oh, him. We called him 'Catcher'. He loved catching balls. He was also a very good herding dog, just like Lucky's going to be. I was just too busy with other things to train him properly." She stopped. When I looked up, she had a faraway dreamy look on her face. "I think he would have been a winner in herding trials," she mused.

I finished pinning the leg but measured it once more just to be sure: twelve centimetres. It was correct. I picked up the scissors and started cutting around the leg.

"You notice how much Lucky has grown since you got him?" Grandma asked. "He's turning into a beautiful dog as well."

She was right. He didn't look all out of proportion any more, and his black coat was becoming glossy and a bit wavy. The hair on his tail was growing longer, so that it fanned when he moved. Even the appearance of the white ring around his eye had improved. It made him look rather distinguished.

"Could you show me some of the signals they use for herding dogs?" I asked. "I'd like to teach him properly."

"I don't know the whistle signals, but we could certainly teach him the verbal ones I know," she said. She was thoughtful for a moment. "You know," she continued, "I bet he would be good at Agility. We could teach him that too."

"What's that?" I asked, continuing to cut.

"Agility is a sport Border Collies usually do well at. It's a series of obstacles that are arranged in a pattern. How fast the dog can complete the circuit and how many mistakes he makes determines the number of points he gets. There are usually Agility trials held here at the end of summer."

"Let's do it," I said, laying the scissors down. "That sounds like fun!"

I held the pants up proudly. "There, that's

finished," I said, heaving a sigh of relief.

Grandma's mouth fell open. "What have you done?" she gasped. She grabbed them out of my hands to look at the legs. Her face drained of colour.

I grabbed them back to look myself. One leg was twice as short as the other! I'd cut the same leg twice!

"Oh no!" I cried, horrified. Grandma slumped back on her stool. I collapsed into a heap on the floor, still holding the pants.

"Can we sew it back on?" I asked hopefully.

"No, I'm afraid not," Grandma said. She held them up against her own waist and looked down. The extra short leg was a bit shorter than the jeans she was wearing.

"You said you had some money saved?"

I nodded slowly. She didn't need to say any more. I'd have to replace them. I'd also have to face Dad to tell him what I'd done.

"I guess we'll have to throw these away," I said glumly.

"Throw them away! Good heavens, no!" Grandma declared. "I'll keep them for myself."

My mouth dropped open. "But they'll be too short even for you. Besides, they're tailored men's pants."

"Seems to me," she retorted, "any length goes

these days for a woman." She quickly laid both pant legs together, smoothed them out, and without measuring or pinning, cut the longer leg to match the shorter.

She held them up gleefully. "There! They might end up looking quite 'classy', as you say." For once I was completely speechless.

"Now, run along and figure out what you're going to say to your dad, while I finish these. I think you've had enough 'sewing' for one day!"

Needless to say, Dad wasn't too pleased, but he didn't get really angry. Maybe it was because between the time I left Grandma and found him, I'd figured out the best way to tell him: "You know those pants you bought today? Well, I'm going to replace them, because something happened while I was learning to hem them."

The outcome of the whole incident as far as Dad was concerned was that he told me I should become a politician, because I have a way of choosing my words to make an ugly situation look quite good. And would I please replace them with one of the other pairs he'd looked at, because he didn't want to appear somewhere wearing the same pants as Grandma.

The outcome as far as Grandma was concerned was that she ended up with her first "new" pair of pants in years. They didn't look "classy" in my opinion, but they did seem to suit her quirky personality.

And the outcome of the whole incident as far as I was concerned was that I wasn't going to be able to get my new bike as soon as I'd hoped. For some reason, my determination to learn to sew was greater than ever. I just had to remember in the future not to talk about Lucky while I was doing it!

17

It was a few days later when we discovered the robin's nest was empty. I couldn't believe how quickly they had grown up and left. Unfortunately, one of them was lying dead at the base of the tree. Perhaps the other four pushed him out, or maybe he'd fallen to his death while learning to fly.

While we were digging a little hole to bury him, Alisha noticed one of the other young robins in a low bush nearby. It didn't display a lot of fear, just hopped and fluttered out of Alisha's grasp as she tried to pick it up.

"I don't think you should try to catch it," Shawn said to her, frowning.

"But it may be hurt," Alisha whispered, stepping back as the little bird crouched and fluttered its wings some more.

"Let's leave it for now. We'll see what Grandma thinks," I suggested.

Grandma was glad we had left it alone. "Its behaviour indicates it was begging for food, so the parents and probably the other babies are still around. They're vulnerable when they first leave the nest, and quite often they don't all survive, but those that do have to learn to be on their own as soon as possible. If I were you, I would just stay away from that area for a while," Grandma advised us.

Plenty of other things happened over the next few weeks to keep my mind off the robins. Grandma showed me how to teach Lucky some basic verbal commands, which he eagerly learned. It made my job with the cows a lot easier.

Rather than riding over, I now usually walked over to get the cows with Lucky at my side. It was great fun to watch the way he handled the whole herd of cows, but particularly Ms. Fancypants. She didn't hang around to argue any more. When she saw Lucky coming, she was usually the first one out the gate, both morning and night.

Lucky loved his job so much that he woke me early every morning by shoving his nose in my face, and every night he sat at the door whining when he felt it was time to go get the cows.

One week Grandma and I, with a little help from Dad, used our imagination to build obstacles similar to what Lucky would face in an Agility Trial. We made jumps of various heights and a high narrow plank to walk along out of lumber left over from Grandma's chicken house. An A-frame structure, on which Lucky would have to run up one side and down the other, was made by hinging together two old pieces of plywood then chaining the bottom together so that it wouldn't collapse unexpectedly. We dragged my old teeter-totter over for a see-saw that he would walk over until it tipped and he could run down the other side. We hung an old tire from a tree for Lucky to jump through and cut twelve pieces of leftover plastic irrigation pipe into one metre lengths, then planted them upright in the ground about forty-five centimetres apart. These were for him to weave his way through. Lastly, we made two different tunnels which he had to run through without being able to see the other end.

At first, no one could think of how to make a rigid, curved tunnel, so we all spent a day or two, while we were putting the other things together, just thinking about it. Then I got the bright idea of taking our four lawn chairs and laying them down in a bit of an curved formation and covering the legs tightly with a tarpaulin, while leaving each end open.

Grandma used her sewing skills and her recycling mentality to make a collapsed tunnel out of my old hula hoop and a set of lightweight, purple flowered floor length drapes she found at the thrift shop for five dollars. They'd been pretty ugly curtains, but when Grandma sewed them together lengthwise and then into a long, long tube which she attached to the hula hoop for the tunnel's entrance, even Lucky must have thought they looked okay, because it wasn't long before this was his favourite part of the course. We put a weight at the other end so that Lucky wouldn't get tangled up in his enthusiasm to make his way through a tunnel he had to open up as he worked his way through. It always made me laugh to see the bump of his body wiggling through that long field of purple flowers. It almost brought them to life and made them look like they were swaying in the wind.

When we introduced Lucky to our course, we put him on a leash and walked him very slowly through each obstacle. Each time he did the right thing, we gave him lots of verbal praise and fed him a little bite of his favourite dog biscuit. It didn't take him long to learn the proper way to complete each obstacle.

Then we set about teaching what "right", "left", "go on straight", "turn around" and "go around" meant. He also had to learn the names of each obstacle so that when he was in the middle of one, he knew which one to tackle next.

Although it appeared as if it were play to

Lucky, I think he loved the challenge of this new learning opportunity. Once he became familiar with each obstacle, he became so excited that he would jump over, under or through whatever he saw next, yipping and yelping, his body hurtling along in a blur. So we also had to teach him the call off signal of "stop", without making him feel he was being reprimanded.

The hardest skill of all to teach him was that when he completed the course, he had to jump onto a platform and sit still until the count of five. At first, he would be so wound up that he would jump over the platform and then circle it twice. Then he got the idea that if he landed on it, he could then jump off and head back through the collapsed tunnel, which was his favourite. The day I got him to land on the platform and sit for the count of five, we were both so excited that I grabbed him in a bear hug and kissed his head, and he licked me on the face.

I put him through the course at least once a day, sometimes twice. Mostly he acted like a hyperactive kid who is so excited that he can't settle down to get a job done properly, but Grandma said he was coming along nicely and that he would probably do well in the August Agility trials, which were rapidly approaching.

I tried to get over to the pond every couple of

days with either Alisha or Shawn, or sometimes just with Ginger and Lucky.

The day Dad was going to drive me into town to get my hair cut, I rode over, Lucky running at our side.

To my surprise, I saw a man wearing a hard hat walking around the perimeter of the pond. I don't think he expected to see anyone. He looked startled as we burst through the bush near him.

"Sorry. I didn't mean to scare you," I said, pulling Ginger to a halt. She put her head down to eat, expecting me to climb down, but we didn't have time to stop for long. I pulled her head back up.

The man winced. "You did give me a bit of a scare. I thought it might be a bear."

"Is it true that there's a development happening around here?" I asked.

"Sure is," he said, removing his hat to wipe his brow. He began to study the pond again, then unrolled a large paper he was carrying to look at it.

"Why are you here?" I asked, suddenly feeling slightly sick.

His gaze swung back to me again. "I'm not sure what business you have here, young lady. As far as I know, this is private property. Seeing as how you're so interested in what's going on, I guess I can tell you that I'm the engineer who's been sent out to figure out the best way to fill in this pond."

"Fill in the pond!" I shrieked, causing Ginger to jump and Lucky to bark. "But you can't fill in this pond!"

He looked at me as if I were insane. "The pond affects the size of these four lots," he said poking his finger at the plans. "It has to be filled in." I stared at the paper. It showed a grid of neat rectangular lots and no pond anywhere.

"But there's a family of turtles living in the pond," I babbled. I had never in my wildest dreams considered this possibility as part of the development.

"I'm sorry," the man said, not looking sorry at all. "You're talking to the wrong person. I've just been hired to do a job, not to decide whether it should be done or not."

"Well, who can I talk to then?" I asked him, my voice rising.

He looked up at me again, his jaw set. "There's no one you can talk to, as far as I'm concerned. Look, kid, it's just a pond…" He began rolling up his plans.

There were so many more things he needed to be told—how the mallards quacked with joy and their feet made a "swilling" sound, skimming onto the pond in spring when they returned home from the south. How frogs and garter snakes nestled in the muddy shores to keep from scorching in the summer sun. How the leaves of the birch trees around the pond's edge rattled and chattered and turned a burnished gold as they welcomed fall. And how, in winter, the overlapping tracks of quail and rabbit and coyote quilted the snow with stories. Lastly, I needed to tell him how you could sit for endless hours watching a family of turtles stack themselves one on top of the other to bask in the sun as if it were the most important thing in the world to do.

But I didn't.

I turned Ginger, and without another word, I urged her into a gallop towards home. I was glad she knew the way and that I could trust her, because tears blinded my vision so that I couldn't see where we were going.

Dad was deep in thought as we drove into town. I don't think he had expected to hear that the pond was to be filled either. For the first time, he too seemed to be concerned, although we didn't talk about it. What was there to say?

I'm sure the lady who cut and styled my hair thought I was in a trance or that there was something weird about me. I just wasn't interested in chatting or laughing at her little jokes. I hardly saw the new image of me as she held up the mirror when she was finished. All I could see in my mind's eye were my little turtles trying unsuccessfully to escape as tons of earth were dumped upon them.

"Looks good," Dad said, eyeing my new haircut when he picked me up.

"Thanks," I said, sighing. I rolled down the window and let the wind sweep and tousle my short curls. I realized we weren't taking the normal route home. "Where are we going?" I asked. I wasn't in the mood for any "Let's cheer Nikki up" antics.

"I think we should stop by the Planning Department to see about the Watson's Pond Development," he said matter of factly as he swung into the parking lot. "I'm going to let you do the talking, Nikki, as you know what questions you want answers to. I'll go with you though."

For the first time, I felt a glimmer of hope. Maybe there had been a mistake. Maybe the developer was doing something he shouldn't. Surely, there had to be rules to protect defenseless animals.

My hopes were quickly dashed.

"I'm sorry, but in this case our hands are tied," the planner explained, shaking his head in sympathy after we'd poured over the map of the area and he'd checked the paper work on file. "Everything is in order. The owner of the property has gone through all the necessary steps to begin development. That pond is his to fill in as he likes."

"But those turtles are becoming endangered," I explained patiently. "I talked to the local wildlife people when I was doing research on the Western Painted Turtle for a school assignment. They told me their habitat is disappearing, and they'll soon be on the endangered list."

"That's right. She did find that fact out," Dad said from behind me. He stepped beside me. "Nikki did a lot of work on that assignment. Her research was very thorough!" From the way the planner was looking at him, I guess Dad decided he'd better explain further. "I was Nikki's teacher as well as her father. That's how I know she did a lot of work, and that her research was thorough." He put his arm around my shoulder and gave me a squeeze. "She got an A on that assignment!" he said rather loudly.

The planner gave me a small smile. "Congratulations," he said.

Dad leaned forward on the counter, "Look, isn't there anything we can do about this? It's obvious that what's about to happen is not right."

The planner shrugged, shook his head and

sighed. "I'm afraid not," he said, closing the file and rolling up the map to indicate our discussion was finished. "As I said before, everything has been done properly. Our hands are tied."

Neither Dad nor I spoke on the way home. I could tell he was upset, but I wasn't sure if it was because the planner hadn't seemed to be overly impressed with my research, or if he were upset about the injustice of it all. I don't really know what he was thinking. All I knew was that somehow I was going to have to stop them from filling in that pond.

18

My first thought was that Grandma would know what to do. She was reading a letter and was deep in thought when I burst through the door.

"Your hair looks nice," she said, looking up.

I ran my hands through it. "Yeah, I guess so," I said. Then I poured out the events of the whole afternoon.

"What can we do to stop them from filling in the pond?" I asked miserably.

Grandma laid the letter down with deliberation and looked at me thoughtfully for a few moments. "It sounds like there isn't much that can be done at this point," she said quietly.

"But there must be some way we can fight it. You've been through this before. You must know what to do."

She shook her head. "I'm afraid the fight is all gone from me. I guess I burned myself out a bit in Australia." She sighed. "You can only butt your head up against ignorance for so long before you've had enough. Besides," she said, picking the letter up again, "I've got this to think about."

I slumped into a chair nearby. "What's that?" I asked.

"It's an offer from some good friends who live on a little island off the coast. They're asking if I'm interested in looking after their small farm for a couple of years while they go overseas."

Her words took a moment to register. "Are you going to do it?" I asked slowly.

She tapped the letter against her hand. "I'm thinking it's maybe time to move on," she said.

"But it's as if your home is here now," I said lamely. "How will you manage by yourself?"

Grandma looked past me. "I can't stay here forever. I knew that when I came." She tapped the letter again and sighed. "I'd be lonely for a while, but I'd learn to manage." She smiled and looked at me. "They even have a few token sheep that would remind me of Australia. I'll have to think about it some more," she said, folding up the letter and putting it in her shirt pocket.

"When would you have to go?" I asked, thinking of the Agility Trial which was coming up in a couple of weeks. Grandma seemed to read my mind.

"Don't worry," she said. "I wouldn't have to go

for nearly another month. Besides, we've both worked too hard with Lucky for me to go without seeing how he does in that trial."

I felt angry and let down for the rest of the day. Neither Shawn nor Alisha was home, so I couldn't share my fears with them. Dad had done what he could by taking me to the Planning Department. He had probably already accepted the fact that the fate of the pond was out of our hands. I knew Mom would think the same way. Grandma, who had been my last resort, was, for once, too busy thinking about other things. I suddenly realized I was upset about the idea of Grandma leaving as well.

I lay in my room with Lucky and tried to read a book, but found that I wasn't even aware of what I was reading. I took Lucky out and ran him through the Agility course, but he seemed to sense my depression, and his heart just wasn't in it.

Purple clouds began to gather once again in the west, this time accompanied by the ominous far off rumbling of thunder. I decided to go and get the cows a bit early so that they'd be back at their own home before the storm hit. Since Lucky was so good at it now, we just walked over rather than taking Ginger. My job now consisted of opening the two gates and giving Lucky the go-ahead. He did the rest by himself.

As we finished and started back for home just before dinner, a loud crack of thunder overhead made me jump. Big, fat raindrops splattered onto us. Lucky cocked his head and whined.

"Come on, Lucky. Let's get home," I called, breaking into a run. He looked up at me and barked his answer. As he ran along beside me, his tail waving in the wind and rain, he seemed to enjoy the storm. Maybe he was tired of the heat and glad it was being washed away, just as I was.

By the time we got home, we were both wet to the skin. I got doubly soaked when I let Lucky in the basement door, and he stopped in front of me and shook himself thoroughly. The wind and thunder passed quickly, but the rain settled into a steady drizzle that continued throughout the night.

19

You know how you wake up sometimes, and you know you're unhappy about something, but it takes a few minutes for it to sink in? That's the way it was the next morning. I slept in late for once, waking before Lucky. A cool breeze wafted in through the open window, and the fresh air smelled damp. I stared at the ceiling for a minute, trying to figure out what was bugging me, then I thought about Grandma possibly leaving. I was just beginning to appreciate the kind of person she really was. Even Mom and Dad didn't seem to mind having her around as much as when she had first come. Did they know she was thinking of leaving?

Then my thoughts shifted to the pond and its seemingly hopeless situation. Suddenly, I had a feeling that something bad was about to happen. I jumped out of bed and began dressing. Lucky, who had been stretched out alongside me enjoying the cooler air, now sensed my urgency.

He jumped off the bed and ran to the door to be let out.

Grandma was surveying her garden. "You sure slept in," she said, glancing up as Lucky ran over to say hello, and I stood rubbing my eyes. "It's nearly nine o'clock. Your mom and dad had to go to town." She leaned on the hoe. "That was some rain we got! I was going to work in the garden, but it's too muddy," she said, poking at the wet ground with the hoe.

"Well, at least the cows will be happy," I said. "They didn't like the heat very much. I'd better get going. They'll think I've forgotten them."

"Have some breakfast first," Grandma called after me.

"I will. Lucky needs his too," I answered.

We ate quickly, then ran out to Ginger. My earlier premonition urged me to ride Ginger bareback again rather than taking the time to saddle her.

The cows knew I was late. They stood waiting for me, mooing and switching their tails. When I opened the gate, Ms. Fancypants was the first out, and the others eagerly followed. They were so anxious to get to the pasture at our place that Lucky didn't have much of a job to do, but we followed along behind them until they were all inside the pasture, and the gate was locked behind them.

"Come on, Lucky, we're going to the pond," I called, turning Ginger sharply and touching her sides with my heels. She leapt into a canter. Clods of mud flew into the air from her feet as we flew along the muddy path. Lucky ran ahead of us, his head low, ears swept back. He seemed to know we were on a serious mission—perhaps he too shared my sense that something was wrong.

I heard it before I saw it. The loud roar of heavy machinery. I bent low and urged Ginger into a gallop. As we neared the large birch, I gasped. A mountain of dirt and rock already sat at the edge of the pond, and a huge loaded dump truck was backing through the brush towards it. Behind sat a bulldozer, its diesel engine sending sickly grey smoke into the air.

I pulled hard on the reins and slid off Ginger's back almost before she skidded to a stop. I quickly laced the reins around a branch and pulled them tight. As I ran for the other side of the pond, all I could hear was the warning "beep beep" of the truck and the sound of breaking branches as it backed slowly through the brush. The engineer I'd spoken to yesterday stood behind the truck signalling it towards the pile.

"Stop!" I shouted as I ran, waving my arms so that I would be noticed over the din of the machinery. I stopped between the truck and the man and turned to face him. "Stop!" I hollered again.

Surprise flew across his face. Then, when he recognized me, he scowled. He held up his hand to the truck, but it had already stopped.

"What are you doing here?" he demanded, glowering at me.

"I...I..." Words suddenly failed me. I fought to gain control because I knew if I burst into tears at this point, all would be lost. Swallowing hard, I blinked back the tears. "Please stop. You don't understand about the pond..." Lucky sat, pressed against my legs whining.

The engineer's face was hard. "I told you before, this is a development on private property. You've no business here. Now come on, move aside!" He stepped out of the way of the truck, waving it past, and I meekly followed. Once he made sure I was out of the way, he walked towards his truck.

I'd failed! I'd done everything I could. This was private property, and I knew that legally, he was right. I had no right to be on it at all.

I stood stiffly, watching as the box of the huge truck lifted high in the air. Then a loud rumbling, which seemed to go on forever, and several tons of rock and dirt and mud crashed onto the ground and into the water of the pond. The box hissed its way back down, and with a wave from the driver, the truck lumbered forward on its way out for another load. Black smoke puffed into the air as the bulldozer revved its engine and moved to move slowly forward.

I looked over my shoulder at the pond and gasped. There on the floating log sat the family of turtles. They must have come up to enjoy the sunshine after the night of rain. Usually, they sit motionless, their eyes closed as they soak up the sun. Now their heads were up looking around. One by one they plopped into the water, soon to be their muddy grave, unless I could prevent it.

Suddenly, the vision of my spirit crab floated into my head, and I knew what had to be done. For the turtles' sake, I couldn't give up! I was going to be as tenacious as that giant crab in my vision and not let go of what I knew was right.

I ran to the huge pile of dirt, Lucky beside me. We scrambled up it, our feet sinking into the loose dampness, my shoes filling with muddy dirt. I grabbed at an exposed branch and pulled myself to the top. As I faced the bulldozer's monstrous yawning bucket chugging towards me, my legs began shaking, and I sank down on a nearby rock. Lucky sat beside me, whining as he watched the advancing bucket loom closer and closer. My heart felt as if it had jumped into my mouth. What was I doing? We could both be killed!

The engineer ran towards the bulldozer, shouting at the driver to stop. The driver peered around the bucket and saw me. With a screech, the machine ground to a halt. The driver jumped out, his arms waving in the air.

"Are you crazy?" he shouted. "You could have been killed! Get off of there!"

I stood up. Lucky stood beside me, the hair on his neck bristling. I looked at both angry faces beneath me and tried to keep my voice from quivering.

"I'm not moving! I'm staying here until I know this pond won't be filled in," I said, suddenly knowing it to be true.

"Why you...you'll move when I get up there," the driver threatened as he started up the hill towards us.

Lucky jumped in front of me, planting all four feet in an attack position. His tail fanning the air, his head held low, a threatening growl crept from his throat. For a moment, I almost laughed. I didn't look at Lucky, but I just knew he was fixing them with the same stare he used on Ms. Fancypants. It said: "Don't fool with me or you'll be sorry!"

"Hang on, Frank," the engineer called. "I'll

phone Mr. Watson. My patience has run out too, but we don't want a lawsuit on our hands for manhandling a kid."

I collapsed back onto the rock as they retreated. The engineer headed to his nearby truck for his cell phone. The driver of the bulldozer stomped back to his machine to turn it off. Avoiding looking my way, he lit up a cigarette.

"Thanks, Lucky," I whispered, stroking his silky neck. Leaning against my legs, he panted, his eyes smiling.

Bits of the phone conversation with Mr. Watson floated through the still air to me: "Pond...wild kid...turtles...bulldozer...dog," were words I could pick out. Then his voice rose. "I don't care if you aren't close by. If you want this pond filled in on time, you'd better get here as fast as you can."

I chewed my lip. I didn't know what would happen when Mr. Watson arrived, but I was going to need help. I fingered Grandma's gold chain for a moment, then carefully undid the clasp. Winding it around Lucky's collar a few times, I did up the clasp so it wouldn't fall off, and left the medallion dangling down Lucky's chest far enough so that Grandma would be sure to see it.

Taking Lucky's face in my hands, I looked him in the eyes. "Grandma! Go find Grandma and bring her back," I said slowly and clearly. His eyes told me he understood.

I released him. "Go!" I shouted, pointing towards home. Barking, he disappeared down the hill, around the edge of the pond and onto the trail. All I could see was the white tip of his tail flashing in a circle as he ran wildly towards home.

Hugging my knees, I breathed a sigh of relief. A breeze picked up, and the sun disappeared behind some thick grey clouds. I shivered, realizing now that I'd been foolish to wear shorts and a T-shirt. A moment later, big fat raindrops began to splatter onto me. The rock I was sitting on felt very hard, I was thirsty, and I began to feel like I had to go to the bathroom.

The rain came in sheets, and both men hastily climbed into the truck. They sat watching me through the rain as they held a seemingly heated debate.

My short, curly hair plastered itself to my head, and rivulets of rain ran into my eyes, down my face and dripped off my chin. The rain pounded into the loose soil around me, turning it into a quagmire of mud. I watched Ginger, still tied to the tree, hunch her back up and tuck her tail between her legs. She shifted as much as she could, so that the storm was coming at her from behind. It was hitting me head on, but I wasn't about to turn away.

I began to feel very miserable and very alone. Then I thought about my spirit crab. "Don't give in, and forget about having to go to the bathroom," it seemed to tell me. I started saying that phrase to myself over and over again. But talking about having to go to the bathroom so much was really making it worse, so I cut that part out. I concentrated on, "Don't...give...in, don't...give...in!" for what seemed to be an eternity.

Slowly, the rain began to let up. Then it stopped. In the hushed silence that follows a storm, before the birds start singing again, I could hear Lucky's excited yipping.

I stood up, stiff and cold. My feet almost disappeared into the mud. "Grandma! Over here," I yelled, waving my arms as she appeared, huffing and puffing behind Lucky. She was carrying an umbrella in one hand and my jacket in the other.

She stopped at the bottom of the dirt pile to catch her breath. She looked up at me. "You're sure a sight! Other than being soaking wet, are you all right?"

I nodded, too emotionally drained to say anything else. Lucky galloped up the hill through the mud and into my arms. I hugged him tightly, choking back tears of relief. Then he shook himself, splattering me with muddy water, and I had to laugh.

"Thought something like this must've happened," she said, shaking her umbrella and folding it up, "when that rascal of a Lucky appeared wearing your gold chain. He made it very clear that I was to come back with him as fast as I could. I had a hard time grabbing your jacket, my umbrella and leaving a note."

The men, seeing Grandma, got out of the truck. "Finally, someone to talk some sense into this girl," the engineer said, stepping forward. "She's wasted a lot of our time. She's acting very irresponsibly!"

Grandma turned to face them. "Is that so! Acting irresponsibly! Well, I guess that depends on which viewpoint you agree with. Me? I'm on her side." She turned her back to them and started clambering up the muddy pile of dirt, her feet making a squishy, slurping sound with each step.

The engineer's mouth fell open. "Oh, for Pete's sake!" he moaned. "I don't believe this. Now we've got two of them!"

I reached my hand out to Grandma and hauled her up. She squeezed my hand. "Don't let go. It's a way of showing solidarity," she whispered with a mischievous smile. With her free hand, she threw the jacket she'd brought around my shoulders. Then we stood, hand in hand, with Lucky between us and faced the men.

"The point you're missing," Grandma said loftily, "is that this young lady is thinking of more than just herself, which is fairly unusual in today's world. She's standing up for what she believes is right!"

"Well, she just about got killed doing it," the engineer muttered. Grandma's hand tightened on mine, and I felt a tremble move through her, but she kept her eyes on the men.

"For your information..." she began.

"The owner of the pond is on his way, Grandma," I interrupted. "Let's wait to talk with him. This fellow doesn't have the authority to stop what's happening. Besides, he doesn't want to hear what we have to say."

The engineer's face began to turn red. "You ladies better make yourselves comfortable if you can. You may be there for a while!" he said in a steely voice before he turned and marched back to his truck.

"Now what do we do?" I asked Grandma.

"Well, I'm going to sit down, and I suggest that you do too, as we're likely to be here for some time." She squatted on my rock, and I found a few branches, which I dragged over to sit on.

"The next thing we're going to do is share these peas I picked this morning." She pulled a handful out of her pocket and offered them to me. "It's past lunch time. You must be hungry."

"I'm more thirsty than hungry," I said, splitting the peas and sharing them with Lucky, who seemed to appreciate their sweet flavour.

"I asked your parents to bring water in the note I left them. I also told them to phone Alisha and Shawn and the newspaper."

I laughed. "You thought of everything!"

Grandma smiled. "Well, don't forget, I have done this a few times before."

We finished the peas in companionable silence. The sun came out in full force, and Grandma put up the umbrella again—this time to shade us from the heat. Lucky stretched out and went to sleep.

"What happens if we can't stop this?" I asked after a while. I wasn't sure what Mom and Dad could or would do to help, or how they'd feel about what I'd done. I remembered the math test incident and what Dad had said about rules and consequences. He lived by rules, and he expected others to do so as well. Most likely he'd tell me I had to respect private property and leave.

Grandma thought for a moment. "The reality is that we may not stop this, Nikki. Sometimes it's impossible to stop things that we think are wrong. Then what you have to do is focus on the fact that you stood up and fought for what you truly believed in. Sometimes that makes it easier to accept things you can't change. It makes living with yourself a whole lot easier."

I was quiet.

"Tell me what happened this morning," she said, trying to change the subject. When I told her about my guiding force being a stubborn crab, she smiled. "Nothing wrong with that. Being tenacious will take you a long way in life."

Lucky woke and stretched in the sunshine. Then he scrambled to his feet, his head cocked towards the trail. He started yipping and dancing around. Mom and Dad, Alisha and Shawn and another lady appeared on the trail. Grandma and I stood up, calling to them. The men climbed out of the truck.

Dad was the first to arrive with the others close behind. Everyone was quiet for a moment as he looked up at Grandma and me holding hands, then turned to gaze at the pond. Finally, he turned to the men.

"Is this your daughter?" the engineer asked, indicating me with a wave of his hand.

Dad seemed to straighten up and stand taller. "Yes, this is my daughter...and my mother," he said in a clear, even voice.

"They've held us up for the better part of the day, and we're not impressed. We've got work to do. They're illegally trespassing and could face arrest. Tell them to come down so that we can get back to work."

Dad hesitated. My heart thumped so loudly, I was sure everyone could hear it. Was he going to tell me to come down? Would I have the courage to defy him if he did? I looked at Grandma. She squeezed my hand. Dad looked up at us again, then turned to the engineer.

"I'm sorry. I understand the position you're in and the delay that has been caused. I know this is private property and that prosecution may take place, but..." he turned to us and started to climb the hill, "I'm joining them!"

The engineer watched, disbelief written on his face as Dad, followed by Mom, Shawn and Alisha, carefully picked their way up the mound of dirt.

"Who are you?" he demanded of the lady who remained at the bottom, aiming a camera at the top of the hill.

"I'm a reporter from the local paper. This will make a great human interest story! Now, if you'll excuse me, I've got work to do."

The engineer groaned. A few minutes later, a half-ton truck drove in. "Thank heavens, Mr.

Watson has arrived. This whole thing has become too crazy," he muttered.

Dad and Mom hugged me when they reached the top. Then Dad turned to Grandma. "You'll never change, will you?" he said with a small smile.

"No," she said, smiling back, "but it looks like you finally might be starting to."

I watched in awe as he took my grandmother's hand and stood beside her. It was the first time I'd seen them physically touch one another since her arrival. As Mom took Dad's other hand and stood beside him, Shawn came to me and gave me a quick hug.

"I'm proud of you, Nikki," he whispered before taking my hand and offering his other hand to Alisha, who was floundering around, trying to get a footing. Her pink shorts had become all grubby, and her new runners kept disappearing in the mud. She finally found her balance and smiled at me. The six of us stood in a line holding hands with Lucky at our feet us as Mr. Watson approached the bottom of the hill, and the lady from the newspaper gleefully shot picture after picture.

20

Yawning, I carefully cut around the picture and article from the front page of the newspaper. I was exhausted after yesterday's excitement, and now my throat felt raw.

"'GIRL AND GRANNY PUT LIVES ON LINE TO SAVE TURTLES'" shouted the headlines.

"Here, Grandma. You can add this to your scrapbook," I said, handing it to her.

"Humph!" snorted Grandma as she took the article from me. "Those newspaper people always seem to get their facts mixed up. These headlines should have been yours alone! I didn't come along until after you'd 'put your life on the line', so to speak."

I laughed. "You deserve as much credit as I do. If you hadn't come along, I'm sure I'd have given up."

"No, you wouldn't have." Her eyes lit up. "The point is, we won!" She danced a little jig around the living room.

We had won. Not only was the turtles' home going to be kept safe, it had suddenly changed from a plain old "pond" to being a "lagoon". The development was to be called "Watson Lagoon Estates". It didn't seem to matter that a lagoon is usually connected to an ocean, while this one was hundreds of miles inland in the middle of a forest.

It wasn't that Mr. Watson was Mr. Nice Guy when he arrived. What he may have lacked in niceness, though, he made up for in smarts. He listened to the engineer, who filled him in on the delays and how they had been caused. Then he watched the reporter clicking away with her camera. He listened politely while I read the research paper on the Western Painted Turtle, which Dad had brought. He really seemed to pay attention when he watched the reporter scribbling notes about how the Western Painted Turtle's habitat was being gobbled up by development, and how they'd soon be on the endangered list. But I think the thing that really made up his mind was when I happened to look back at the pond after I'd finished reading my report.

"Look!" I shouted, pointing. Seven turtles had resurfaced and were sitting side by side on their log basking in the warm sunshine. The reporter zoomed in on them, "oohing" and "aahing" as her camera clicked away. I told her they had names, and she scribbled away happily. Shawn didn't argue about the names, even though he knew that I didn't know one turtle from another. I was quickly learning how politics work, and I was going to use everything I could to my advantage.

Mr. Watson knew when to give in. His name was well known around the area. He simply could not afford to appear on the front page of the newspaper as an ogre, bent on destroying the home of a family of turtles who all had names. Besides, as Dad pointed out, why not take advantage of the situation? Why not make those four lots smaller and more expensive because they bordered the pond—excuse me, I mean the "lagoon", as Mr. Watson quickly corrected him.

So, by the time we climbed wearily off that mountain of dirt, we were all satisfied. I wouldn't have the area to ride in any more, but at least the pond and the turtles would be safe, so I was happy. Since Mr. Watson appeared to "save" the pond, he took on the appearance of a bit of a hero. That probably made him happy, much I'm sure as Dad's suggestion to charge more for the waterfront lots did. Even the engineer and the driver of the bulldozer seemed satisfied. Now they had more work to do. The mountain of dirt had to be removed, and a new design for the incorporation of the "lagoon" had to be devised.

"Nikki?" I shook myself back to the present. I could tell from the tone of Grandma's voice that she had something serious to tell me.

"I've decided to take that farmsitting job at the end of the month."

I bit my lip, suddenly realizing how big a chunk of my life she had become. "I'll miss you," I said quietly.

"I know. I'll miss you too, but yesterday I realized a few things about myself."

I looked up. "Like what?" I asked.

"Well," said Grandma, "I've been a little bit like one of those baby robins. You and your mom and dad provided me with a safe haven—kind of like a nest, when I needed it. But what happened yesterday made me aware that I still want to fight for the things I believe in. Like the robins, I need to learn to be on my own as soon as I can." She sighed. "I'm not getting any younger, you know."

"Have you told Mom and Dad yet?"

Grandma smiled. "Yes. They understand. They're probably quite relieved, if the truth be known."

I frowned. "Don't be silly. Of course, they're not."

"Ever since your dad was a little boy, we've just sort of rubbed along together—seeing most things from different sides. It can't have been easy for any of you, my being here." She looked away, deep in thought.

Suddenly, she appeared older and a little frail. She was right on all accounts. It was time for her to be on her own while she was still able, and at times it hadn't been easy having her. But that was before I'd really got to know her. Now I would worry about her.

"Come on, Grandma," I said to cheer us both up. "Let's go run Lucky through the course. We haven't got much time left to work with him."

I didn't know it then, but that was the last time I would work with him for the next two weeks, because I became sick and ended up in bed with a terrible cold which threatened to turn into pneumonia.

21

The day of the Agility Trials I woke early. I still didn't have much energy and my head ached, but we'd worked too hard for this, and I wasn't about to miss it. Even though I'd missed a lot of practise time with Lucky, I was confident that he would do well.

Mom and Grandma fussed over me during breakfast. Grandma, with Lucky's help, had taken over the job of moving the cows back and forth. Grandma insisted she would do it by herself today while I practised with Lucky one more time before we had to leave for town around noon.

Lucky jumped in circles around me as we walked to the course we'd set up. Even though Grandma had run him through it a few times, he knew I was the one he should be working with. Dad, who had come to watch, was impressed with the speed and accuracy Lucky displayed as he raced through the course, yipping with joy. He was equally impressed when Lucky was able to sit at the end through the count of five. As we walked back to the house, Lucky leapt ahead, barking. Every few seconds he'd look over his shoulder to make sure I was following.

"I think he's missed working with you," Dad said, laughing.

Mom met us at the door. "Grandma isn't back yet. We should go soon." She looked at Dad. "Why don't you drive over and pick her up? Maybe the cows gave her some trouble when she showed up without Lucky. We'll be ready when you get back."

I doubted that the cows had given Grandma any trouble. Lucky had them in such a routine now that I was sure they would just automatically move out and down the road by themselves once the gate had been opened. If I'd have thought otherwise, I'd have gone with her.

By the time Dad got back, we were standing outside waiting. I'd even had time to give Lucky a quick brushing so that his coat was all smooth and lustrous. I could tell when they drove in that something was wrong. Grandma's face was grey and etched with pain. Dad looked very sober.

"What happened?" I cried, running to the car.

"I tripped over a rock and twisted my ankle. That's all. I'll be fine," Grandma said.

"You're as white as a ghost, Iris," Mom said, coming up beside me. She peered in the car window. "Look at that ankle. It's twice its normal size!"

"She can't walk. It's either a bad sprain, or even worse, it could be broken," Dad said.

Grandma winced. "It's just a sprain. I'll be okay."

"Come on, everybody. Get in. I'll drop you off at the fairgrounds, then I'll take Mom to Emergency."

"I can't miss seeing how Lucky and Nikki do," Grandma protested.

"Oh, yes, you can. For once, I'm going to insist that you do as I say. We're not going to take any chances with that ankle," Dad said sternly as Mom and Lucky and I piled into the back seat.

I leaned forward. "Dad's right. You need to go to the hospital. I promise to tell you all about it."

She leaned her head against the seat and closed her eyes. "I guess you're right," she said faintly.

•   •   •

The fairgrounds were full of activity and people. I didn't want Lucky to get over-stimulated from all the sounds and smells that were new to him, so we skirted the midway and headed straight for the large grassy area behind, where the Trial would be held.

Mom said she'd go get us a burger while I sat with Lucky to keep him calm, but I told her that I wasn't hungry. My stomach was doing flip-flops. She went to get her own hamburger while Lucky and I watched the course being set up. It also gave us an opportunity to size up our competition.

Five other dogs were listed in the show book we'd been mailed. As I looked around, I could locate all of them in various places, waiting and watching like I was.

A German Shepherd—probably not quite fast enough because of his size, a Scotch Terrier—legs too short, a tri-coloured Sheltie—a herding breed which loved competitive shows (we might have trouble beating this one), and two dogs whose breed I couldn't identify. Probably mongrels. Sometimes a mongrel proved to be the best dog for whatever reason. At least Lucky was the only Border Collie, and I knew from the reading I'd done that this breed was well known for its agility and speed.

Mom returned with her burger. It was obvious that Lucky hadn't lost his appetite from nerves! With great enthusiasm he gobbled down the bits Mom tore off for him.

Our event was called. Lucky and I went to

hear the judge read the rules:

—Refusal of any obstacle will result in a loss of points

—Knocking down of any jump will result in loss of points

—All spokes of the weaving strand must be woven in one direction

—Any obstacle taken out of sequence will result in a loss of points

—Dog must sit on pedestal, untouched by trainer, for a count of five when course is finished

—Course must be completed within specified time

We were to be fourth in running the course. I hoped Lucky would learn from watching the others before him, as the course was configured slightly differently from the way we'd set ours up. However, he became so excited when the Scottie started meticulously going through the obstacles, that I could hardly calm him down. I guess he couldn't stand to see it done so slowly. I became embarrassed as Lucky danced around on the leash, barking and whining. I finally took him down the field away from the competition for a walk, but he kept looking over his shoulder and getting excited all over again.

I sat down with him and held him close for a minute. As soon as I let him go, he turned, and, dropping into the herding crouch, he fixed his eyes on every move the next two dogs went through. I could tell from a distance that the Shepherd was slower than we would be, but I wasn't sure if he'd run a clean circuit. We watched the third dog, one of the mongrels, as we walked back. He was fast, but too excitable. Twice, not listening to his trainer, he went the wrong way and lost points.

Then it was our turn. I bent to unsnap the leash and eyeballed Lucky. "Be good. Stay calm and listen!" Then the judge blew her whistle, and Lucky was off in a streak of black and white.

He cleared the first two jumps quickly and easily and ran along the narrow plank as we'd practised over and over. Then he fairly flew through the tire hoop. As he whipped around the obstacles and over the jumps, he barked in a frenzy. He ran up the teeter-totter, and, not waiting for the board to tip the other way before going down like most dogs do, he leapt from the top and forced the board down. He and the board hit the ground at the same time. Then he was off to the A-frame structure.

The crowd, standing and sitting behind ropes

around the perimeter, began to laugh and cheer at his speed and enthusiasm. I was afraid he wouldn't hear my commands.

When he got to the A-frame, he faltered for a split second—it was turned in a different position than the one that we had at home.

"Left!" I shouted, pointing. "Go left!" He heard me. Without looking my way, he veered around the structure, ran up the left side and down the other side.

Lucky always had the most fun with the collapsed tunnel. This consists of a hoop on edge as an entry point, and then a eight metre-long tube of parachute cloth which only opens up as the dog works his way through it. Now, as the crowd watched him disappear into the hoop and a bump snake its way through the tube, they laughed and cheered even harder.

The last obstacle was weaving the spokes. When a dog is too excited, it's easy to make mistakes. They might miss a spoke and take a short cut just to be done with the whole thing.

"Steady, Lucky, steady!" I shouted, even though I hadn't taught him what that meant. The tone of my voice must have given meaning to the word. He wove his way through each spoke quickly without missing any.

Then he ran to the pedestal, where I was

waiting. He leapt on top and sat through the count of five with his tongue hanging out and his eyes shining. When he heard "five", he leapt off the box into my arms. The crowd went wild!

What can I say? The other mongrel and the Sheltie were good, but I knew the first place ribbon was ours. When the judge called our name, we ran over to her. She shook my hand and handed me the beautiful blue rosette ribbon. When I bent to show Lucky, he playfully took it in his mouth and raced around the ring once more, much to the further delight of the crowd. I found Mom, and we retrieved the ribbon before it got chewed on.

"You're quite a crowd pleaser, Lucky," Mom said after congratulating us.

I agreed. "I think that's what made him work so well. He loved the sound of the crowd!" We found a shady spot and gave him a drink of water. I laid back in the grass with Lucky curled up beside me.

"Nikki?" It was the judge. I sat up quickly. Don't tell me there's been a mistake, and Lucky hasn't taken first place after all, I thought.

She smiled at us. "I just wanted to tell you how much I enjoyed watching Lucky compete. You've trained him very well." She crouched to stroke him. "He's still young. I hope you'll continue training and showing him. I think he has Champion potential."

I thanked her before she left to judge another class. Mom suggested I lie back down to rest. She covered me with her jacket, even though it was a warm day. I guess mothers always worry when you've been sick, no matter how old you are.

I was feeling a little weak after all the excitement, but I found it hard to rest. Finally, we got up and went to the entrance of the fairgrounds to wait for Dad and Grandma, who didn't arrive for some time.

They both looked tired when they picked us up. Grandma's ankle had suffered a bad sprain. She would be on crutches for the next three weeks at least. Her foot was all bandaged and still twice its normal size, but the pain left her face when she heard about Lucky's afternoon.

"I knew you'd do it!" she said, stroking Lucky, who wagged his tail.

I told her what the judge had said to me. "I'm glad you won't be able to go to the island now. When I go back to school, your ankle will be nearly better again, and you can work with him lots," I said.

"Oh, I'm still planning on going," Grandma said. "I promised them I'd come, and since they're leaving the country, I have to go when I said I would," Grandma said matter of factly. "My ankle will do a lot of healing in the next two weeks."

Dad chewed his lip. "One of us could stay with you for a few days if it weren't so close to school starting again."

Grandma smiled. "I'll manage fine. I won't do anything I can't. Besides, they've got neighbours who will help me if I need it."

We all knew that once Grandma had made up her mind, there was no use trying to change it. She would manage somehow, because she said she would! Looking after her garden for her and working with Lucky over the next couple of weeks gave me time to do a lot of thinking.

22

W ell, here we are," Grandma said brightly as we stood in the middle of the little farmhouse. Mom and Dad walked through the kitchen, living room and tiny bedroom without saying anything. Their silence spoke volumes!

With a lot of persuasion Dad had convinced Grandma to wait two more weeks until she was at least off her crutches. He had arranged for neighbours to look after the place until Grandma arrived. This had brought us into the first week of school, so this weekend was to be a quick trip to the island and back.

"Where's the bathroom?" I asked, as Lucky and I followed along.

"It's an outhouse. Probably out back," Grandma said.

Dad's eyes roamed from the stained old wallpaper to the worn couch to the wood stove. "Who are these friends of yours, anyway?"

"Now, don't go getting on about my friends.

They're good people. They just decided long ago to get out of the rat race and quit their city jobs. As a result, they don't have much."

"That's obvious," Dad said, poking around the wood stove. "Well, at least this looks fairly new and safe." He looked out the window. "They've left you a good stack of wood as well."

"You've got to admit, the view makes up for what the house lacks," Grandma said as we all gazed out the window. White sails skipped across the blue water of the nearby harbour. The road leading down to the ferry was framed by hills covered with trees of gold and red. She opened the kitchen door. "Look, I've even got my own veranda to enjoy it from."

"There's the outhouse, Nikki," Dad said, pointing out back to a tiny shingled building with an artistic moon cut out of the door.

"And there are the sheep," I cried. Four black-faced sheep nibbled at grass in a small pasture beside the outhouse. Lucky peered around the corner, and his ears perked up. He woofed.

"I'll get the crate of chickens and settle them into their house. Then I'm afraid we have to get back into that ferry line-up," Dad said as he looked at the cars starting to form a queue at the harbour.

"I'll get your bags of vegetables," Mom said. I

started to follow, but Grandma called me back.

"Nikki, there's something I want to give you," she said. She grabbed the cane she still had to use and hobbled over to her backpack. I watched as she rummaged through it and pulled out her scrapbook. "I want you to have this," she said handing it to me.

"I can't take your scrapbook. It shows all your accomplishments. It contains all your memories. You can't give them away," I said.

"Oh, I'll always have the memories." She got a faraway look in her eyes. "But sometimes, in order to go ahead, you have to stop dwelling on the past." She looked at me, smiling. "Besides, there are still some empty pages to fill. I have a feeling that someday you'll be filling them."

I held the book close to me. She had indeed brought me a beautiful book, just as I'd told Alisha long ago. I just didn't know it at the time.

Mom and Dad came back into the house. "The ferry traffic looks heavy. I'm going to have to get the car in line, even though we won't be leaving for a while," Dad said.

He walked to Grandma, and they stood awkwardly looking at each other for a moment. Then he gathered her in his arms and held her tightly for a moment. "Take care of yourself, Mom. We'll visit often. Remember, we're only a six hour drive away, so if you really need us, please call."

"Can I walk on, Dad?" I asked. "I'd like to stay a few more minutes with Grandma."

Dad checked his watch. "As long as you're there in the next fifteen minutes," he said.

"I will be, I promise."

Mom gave Grandma a hug as well and repeated what Dad had said about coming for visits.

"Come on, Kay. Bye, Mom. Don't be long, Nikki," Dad said before he closed the door.

Lucky sat down at my feet, whining, as if he knew something was about to happen that concerned him. My heart started pounding. I took a deep breath. "I have a gift for you too, Grandma," I said. She looked at me in surprise.

"I want you to have Lucky," I said evenly, handing her his leash.

"Lucky? Don't be silly, girl. He's your dog!" she said, backing away.

"Yes, but he loves you too. I'm going to have a very busy year now that I'm in Grade Eight—too busy to spend time with Lucky," I lied. "Besides, my job with the cows is over. He wouldn't have much to do at our place. He can help you here with the sheep."

"What about his Agility training? What about his chances of becoming a Champion?" she asked quietly.

I suddenly realized I hadn't taken Lucky's feelings into consideration. He would miss his training. He would miss me a lot! But Grandma needed someone to look after her and someone to talk to. More importantly, she needed a friend. Lucky would be all of those things to her. I was sure that somehow he would understand why I had given him away—and that he would rise to the occasion.

"There are more ways to be a Champion than by winning prizes, Grandma. You of all people know that."

Her eyes became misty. "You said you never wanted to go through the pain of losing another dog."

"I know," I said slowly, "but there's a difference between losing something, and giving something away."

Grandma clasped her hands in front of her chest as she looked down at Lucky. He whined, looking up at the two of us.

I hate long goodbyes. I looked out the window and checked my watch. "I've got to go."

I knelt in front of Lucky. Taking hold of his dear face, I looked him in the eyes. "Be good. Take care of Grandma." I couldn't bear the thought of hugging him, so I patted the top of his head. His tail thumped the linoleum, and he started for the door, for once not quite understanding what was happening. I held my hand up for him to stay.

I stood up and faced Grandma. Before either of us knew it, we were hugging each other fiercely. "Goodbye, Grandma. Take good care of Lucky." I turned quickly and ran down the driveway without looking back.

I could almost feel him beside me, leaping with joy, his tail fanning against my legs, his excited yip-yipping as we raced for the ferry. My eyes filled with tears, even though what I'd done felt good and right. It wasn't as if I'd never see him again. I planned on coming back on the bus for a visit as soon as I could. The money I'd saved for the new mountain bike would pay for a few bus trips. Nearing the ferry, I dug out a Kleenex from my pocket and blew my nose.

When I found Mom and told her what I'd done, she hugged me tightly. "Oh, Nikki!" was all she said, and her eyes became misty too. Dad looked a little wet in the eyes as well, so I went to stand at the railing as we pulled out of harbour.

"Look!" I called, pointing to shore. "I can see the house. There's Grandma on the veranda." Beside her sat Lucky. I swear he was wagging his tail.

Even though I knew she couldn't see me, I waved until we rounded the bay and were out of sight.